TEMPT

Marie Tuhart

https://www.marietuhart.com/

Tempt, Copyright © 2020 Marie Tuhart
All rights reserved
Print ISBN: 978-0-9971800-5-3
Digital ISBN: 978-0-9971800-4-6

Cover design by Designed by D
Editing by Red Quill Editing Services

Learn more about Marie Tuhart and her books at her
website and for up to date information about releases,
please consider joining Marie's mailing list.

QUALITY CONTROL: We strive to produce error-free
books, but even with all the eyes that see the story during
the production process, slips get by. So please, if you find
a typo or any formatting issues, please let us know
at marie@marietuhart.com so that we may correct it.
Thank you!

Dedication

There are several people who guided me through the process of creating this new series and the first book:

Laurie, thank you for all your experiences not only editing but formatting.

Nia and Isabel, my critique partners who always find ways for me to improve my story.

Red Quill Editing, for guiding me into making the story strong and reminding me not to short change the emotion.

To My Readers:

This book contains elements of the BDSM lifestyle that are only true to life in this book. There are varying forms of the lifestyle as decided between the people involved. While I researched and talked with people in the lifestyle, this is my take on how my character choose to live.

If you decide to explore the lifestyle yourself please remember to always be safe. Never go home with someone you don't know. Attend a munch or a small get-together with people first to see if this is something you want in your life. Reading and living are very different.

Chapter One

Sierra Blake muttered a curse as she traipsed down the side of the road. Damn Carl. Why hadn't she listened to her instincts? If she had, she wouldn't be in this mess, walking beside a deserted road in near-darkness. She adjusted her backpack and kept walking. There was a driveway here, somewhere; she'd seen it when they'd driven out to the campground.

A raindrop hit her nose and she glanced to the dark gray sky. Oh great. While rain wasn't unusual in the Pacific Northwest, the forecast hadn't called for it. This day was about to get worse. Not that the day hadn't been a clusterfuck already. A snort of laughter escaped her lips.

Carl, her now ex-boyfriend, had convinced her to go on this camping trip. No computers, no cell phones, no tablets, nothing. He said it would bring them closer together. Like that really worked. He neglected to tell her they were going to a horror campout.

She hated horror movies and being scared. Carl had made fun of her and laughed. Sierra had barely slept last night, so she was tired, cranky, and wanted to go home. She'd tried all day to convince him, but Carl hadn't listened. He didn't believe her when she said she'd pack up and leave.

It might not have been the brightest idea, but she couldn't stay at that campground another second. She puffed out a breath. It started to rain as she found the driveway. She turned in. She couldn't see a house, but she'd seen a car drive in yesterday, so maybe the house wasn't too far.

Sierra pulled up the hood on her jacket while she continued to walk. She had a light sweater and t-shirt under her jacket. Hopefully, she'd stay dry under her jacket long enough to get to the house. When water dripped onto her face, she let out a sad laugh. Well, maybe not.

Trees lined both sides of the slightly curved, paved driveway. The slight breeze rustled the leaves and the dark shadows reached toward her. Last night, her sleep had been broken several times by screams and maniacal laugher—all fake, but her nerves were fried. She glanced at those trees, afraid someone or something was going to jump out. Sierra shook her head. A ways in, a plain steel gate stood in front of her. At least it was open, so someone must be home. Rain streamed down her face and neck. If she ever saw Carl again, she'd kick him in the nuts for being such an ass.

After she passed the gate, the road widened and gravel crunched beneath her feet. The spiraling pine and fir trees receded. Sierra found herself standing at the base of a very large, well-lit circular driveway. She glanced up at the house—well, actually it was a mansion—outdoor flood lights blazing. Cars, parked in neat rows, gleamed under the lights. Damn! She hoped the owner wouldn't mind the interruption.

She trudged up the two steps to the front door. The big oak door gleamed and had the letters WS carved into the wood. The letters themselves were an aqua-blue color outlined in black. Maybe the owner's initials? She pounded hard against the door. She didn't hear any music, so maybe the party hadn't started yet.

The door opened.

"What the fuck?"

Sierra fought the urge to take a step back at the rough male voice. Blinking the rain out of her eyes, she stared at the bare male chest. Her heart pounded as she allowed her gaze to travel up the sculpted pecs, to unsmiling lips, stormy hazel eyes, straight, medium length black hair and a pair of red devil horns on his head. The man was tall, over six feet.

She swallowed. "Sorry to bother you. If I could borrow your phone, I need to call someone to pick me up."

The man made a noise in the back of his throat. "Ralph," he said over his shoulder, "towels please, and lots of them."

His husky voice sent a shiver down her spine. Must be the rain. He was staring down at her.

"Get in here before you catch a cold."

"But the floors..." She was dripping water from everywhere.

He reached out and took her by the elbow before pulling her into the foyer and slamming the door shut behind them. "Floors can be cleaned. You're shivering." He glanced down at her. "May I?" He gestured to her feet.

She nodded without thinking. He was right; she was soaked and cold. Her gaze shifted as he knelt down and unlaced her boots.

He was wearing dark, well-worn, loose pants and a pair of soft black shoes. Okay, maybe he was afraid she'd stomp on his toes.

"I'm sorry to disturb your party." She ignored the zing of arousal shooting down her spine as his fingers curved around her ankle after removing her boots.

"Party?"

"The horns." She waved toward his head.

He grinned, and her breath caught in her throat.

"Ah, yes. Saints and Sinners party."

Halloween party. She'd totally forgotten Halloween was next week.

Another man, carrying towels, came rushing out of the doorway down the hall. The man in front of her grabbed the top one, shook it out, and offered it to her.

"Thank you." She took the towel and rubbed her face. Warmth enveloped her skin. She bit back a delightful moan. The towels had been heated.

"Take the backpack off." She obeyed without thinking.

Sierra shrugged the pack off and dropped it to the floor, then rolled her shoulders. When did her pack grow so heavy? She didn't have that much in it.

The man shook out another towel and draped it over her shoulders before taking the one in her hands and replacing it with another one. "Ralph, grab one of the robes, please."

"Sure, boss." The man lumbered off.

"That's not necessary. If I could just use your phone."

Her white mesh dress showed off her creamy skin, the white thong she wore, and the nakedness of the rest of her body. Only the halo on her head reminded him of an angel. He bet the men of the club were a little ticked that he pulled her away.

"Yes, Master Max?" She stopped before him, her eyes downcast.

"Regina, Ralph will carry the clothes and pack to the utility room, if you would please wash, dry and fold them. There should be one of my black bags in the room, so once folded, put the clothes into the bag and bring it to my office."

"Yes, Master Max." She glanced at Ralph before making her way down the hall.

"Ralph, please put these on my desk." Max handed Ralph the wallet and keys.

"Sure thing, boss." Ralph took the items from him, then picked up the clothing and pack and strode down the hallway. Max slipped back into the women's bathroom and walked over to the cabinet. He pulled out a fresh robe, and two heated towels.

The water shut off. "I have towels for you."

A small squeak emerged from the shower. Jumpy woman. Not that he blamed her; she was in a strange house with people she didn't know. Taking the first towel, he pushed his hand around the curtain. She took the towel, and he shook out the second one. "Here's another for your hair."

He wondered how long her hair was. It had been braided and disappeared down the back of her shirt.

"Thank you." Her voice was soft. How would that voice sound when she was tied up in his bed?

9

Don't get ahead of yourself. He didn't even know this woman. But from the second he'd seen her on his doorstep, something deep inside of him perked up. A part of him he hadn't felt or seen in a long time. Not since he first met his ex. He froze. *Tread carefully.* He didn't want another mess like that one.

The curtain was drawn back. She'd wrapped the towel around her body, and had her hair somehow in the other one with it twisted on top of her head. He shook his head.

"What?" She tilted her head.

"I have never figured out how women do that thing with the towel." He motioned to the towel covering her hair.

She let out a laugh that caused shivers of anticipation to stream through his veins. Oh yes, Sierra intrigued him and woke his libido. He frowned, then grinned. Maybe she was just what he needed.

"It's something we learn as children."

Max shook his head, and held open the robe for her.

"I thought you were getting my clothes?"

"There's a problem with your clothes." He kept his gaze on her until she let out a sigh and slipped her arms into the robe, shrugging off the towel with her back to him. This time she pulled the robe closed and belted it.

"And what is that?"

"They're soaked."

"What?" She spun to face him. "That backpack is waterproof."

"Maybe water resistant, but not waterproof."

"This night just keeps getting worse and worse."

"Maybe I can improve it." He lifted her as she swayed once again. She was a light thing. She needed more meat on her bones. He couldn't wait to take care of her.

"Why did you pick me up again?"

"Because you're swaying on your feet."

"I am?"

"Yes."

At least she didn't struggle or protest. Maybe he was making progress.

"Where are we going?"

"My office." He turned left out of the women's bathroom and strode down the hallway. Her head swiveled as they walked past the club entrance. The music had changed to a techno-beat. Someone must be doing a flogging.

"That sounds like one hell of a party," she said.

"It is." Max didn't elaborate. At the end of the hall, he opened the door to his office and then sat her on the dark brown sofa. "You told me you walked from the campground."

"Yes." Her blue gaze met his.

"Why?" He wanted the rest of that story.

"Why what?" She crossed her arms over her chest.

Defensive little thing.

He liked it. "That campground is about four miles from here, so why did you walk?"

"That far? No wonder my legs hurt."

Max leaned against his desk and stared at her. She would learn that, when he asked a question, he expected an answer. He waited, studying her with narrow eyes.

"Fine," she burst out. "My now ex-boyfriend thought a weekend camping would bring us closer together, but he didn't tell me it was a horror campout complete with all sorts of gory crap. When he wouldn't take me home, I packed up and left."

His jaw tightened with each word. Give him five minutes with her ex-boyfriend... Max blew out a breath.

"You never told me your name." He didn't want her to know he'd been snooping in her wallet. It wasn't his finest moment, but sometimes a man did something he wasn't proud of.

"Sierra. Sierra Blake."

The name suited her. "Your clothes are being washed and dried; it will probably take about forty-five minutes."

"That wasn't necessary."

"It was." He reached over and picked up his cell phone from where it sat on his desk. "Since I didn't find a cell phone in your pack, I'm assuming you don't have one."

"It was part of the camping trip. No electronics." She glared at him. "You went through my pack?"

"It was soaked." He patted her wallet and keys where they sat on his desk. "Your belongings are safe with me, just as you will always be."

She held his gaze. That was new. Most women he knew lowered their gazes when they tangled with him, but then Sierra didn't quite fit the sub profile.

"You could have brought my pack to me to empty."

"I should have, but I didn't want to interrupt your getting warm, and this way, your clothes are already being taken care of."

"Let the record show I'm not happy about this."

"Noted." Max held his phone out to her. She took it from him and dialed, letting out a loud sigh. "Hey Crys, it's Sierra. I need your help. Can you call me back..." She glanced up at him, and he rattled off his number. Sierra repeated it. "I'm in a jam, and I need you to pick me up. Call when you can." She hit the off button and held his cell out to him. "Thank you. I'm sorry."

He put his finger against her soft lips. "No more apologizing. You are the victim." He took his phone and set it on his desk. His phone would stay here in the office. The club had rules and one of them was no cell phones.

"I've taken you away from your party."

"They'll survive without me." A knock sounded on the door before it was pushed open. Jordan stepped into the room.

His friend was dressed much like him, black pants, and shoes, bare chest. He also wore a pair of devil horns and pointy ears. His black hair was mussed.

"Max, we need you for a moment." Jordan turned his head, and his gaze raked over Sierra.

Sierra put her arms over her stomach and seemed to shrink into herself. Interesting. She didn't do that with him. Max snapped his fingers. "Can't you handle it?" Why did he dislike the way Jordan was looking at Sierra?

Jordan glanced from Sierra to him. "They want you." Jordan's gaze returned to Sierra. "And who is this lovely morsel?"

"Not for you." Max placed himself between Jordan and Sierra. Jordan's eyebrows rose. "I'll be there in a minute." Why was he getting defensive with his friend and silent partner in the club?

Jordan grinned and bowed. "Okay, boss." He turned and left the room.

13

"Boss? Ralph called you that too."

"Jordan's just being a smart ass." He ran a finger over her cheek, enjoying the feel of her soft skin against his. "Will you be okay for a few minutes?"

"I think I can manage." The spunk was back in her voice, and damn if his dick didn't react to it.

"Do you need anything to eat or drink before I go find out what's happening at the party?"

"I'm fine. Thank you."

"Make yourself at home." He turned and left the room. Jordan was waiting for him.

"So, what's her story?" Jordan asked as they walked toward the club.

"She got caught in the storm and needs a ride home."

"Car break down?"

"No car."

"Then how the hell did she get here?" Jordan was frowning.

"Walked from the campground." Max held up his hand. "Short version: Her ex-boyfriend took her camping, didn't tell her it was the horror campout. He refused to take her home, so she packed up and started walking."

"The ex is an asshole."

"Bastard is more like it." Max clenched his hands.

"Why don't we seek this guy out and show him a thing or two about how to treat a lady? I'm sure Damon would enjoy it as well."

Max grinned. Jordan and Damon were his two best friends and silent partners in the club. "I'm sure, but not tonight. Right now my priority is getting her dry and home."

"Are you going to take her?" Jordan asked.

Max shook his head. "She insisted on calling her friend. She's already upset that she's taking me away from my party and I've taken a few liberties that have pushed her buttons. I figure if I try to drive her home, she'll fight me on it."

"No woman fights with Max." Jordan grinned.

"I've done enough already, and I don't want to scare her off permanently." It was the truth. He'd tried to keep his dominant side toned down, but it still came out. It was a natural part of him. He didn't know if she was in the lifestyle and consent was a big thing. He needed to remember that even with his protective instincts on high.

"What's going on?" Jordan leaned toward him.

"I don't know." Max rubbed his neck. From the moment he saw Sierra standing in his doorway, soaking wet with those big blue eyes, something inside him snapped into place. "Besides, she doesn't know about the club, and I wasn't about to tell her tonight."

Jordan nodded. "Will you tell her?"

"If I see her again." Why did his gut tighten at the thought of not seeing her again? "Why do you need me?"

"Walt wants to use the bull whip."

"No." Max ran his hand over his face.

"That's what I told him, but he's insisting on talking to you."

"Fine let's get this done, then I need to get back to Sierra."

"Sure."

Max glanced around his club: *Wicked Sanctuary*. He smiled. The Saints and Sinners party was in full swing. Moans, groans, and cries of pleasure could be heard from various corners. Yes, it was a good night. He wondered how his guest would react if she saw what went on here.

* * * *

Sierra blew out a breath the second the door closed behind Max. Now she understood what women meant when they said "a man's man." Max was that and more. Testosterone flowed from him like ocean waves, and her body reacted.

Weird. She'd never had this kind of reaction around a man before, bossy or not. But with Max, it was different. She wanted to obey him. Sierra shook her head. She wasn't a submissive type of woman. It must be the lack of sleep messing with her mind.

She glanced around his office. The chocolate leather sofa was soft beneath her. An oak desk sat across from her, big and imposing, like the man himself. She stood up. There was a matching five-shelf bookcase and three filing cabinets.

Sierra wandered over to the bookcase. Her gaze took in the books. Computer code? Was it possible Max was a computer geek? No geek she ever knew looked like a Greek god.

She bent down to look at the lower shelves, scanning titles, and one caught her eye. *BDSM For The Novice*. Was Max into BDSM? She reached for the book, then pulled back.

Well, he had said to make herself at home. She slid the book out and carried it over to the sofa. The spine was well worn, like it had been read over and over again. She was curious.

Chapter Two

"So who is the hunk?" Crystal asked as she pulled out onto the main road.

"That was Max." Sierra rested her head against the seat. "What a day."

"I gathered. Tell me what happened."

Sierra told her friend about Carl and the campout. Walking to Max's house, her wet clothes, taking him away from his party. She didn't say how his touch made her tingle inside, let alone what his deep husky voice did to her bones.

"And Max?" Crystal asked.

"What about him?"

"The man was bare-chested, wearing a pair of black pants, and had devil's horns on his head."

Sierra laughed. "You know, after the initial shock of seeing him, I forgot all about the horns. He was hosting a Saints and Sinners party."

"Are you telling me you didn't flirt with that perfect male specimen?"

"Crystal, until earlier today, Carl was my boyfriend."

"Carl was an ass. Max is a delicious hot fudge sundae."

Sierra laughed. "Yes, to both." She turned the card over in her hand. "Thank you for coming to get me."

"I'm sure Max would have driven you home."

"I wasn't going to take him away from his party. It was bad enough as it was." Guilt hit her low in the stomach.

"I'm pretty sure he wouldn't have minded. You said a Saints and Sinners party?"

"That's what Max called it. I really didn't see much. The music had a primal beat, not what I would expect at the party." Sierra glanced at the clock in the dashboard. "Is it really that late?" It was almost ten.

"You called me around seven, I called back at eight forty-five. I was surprised when Max answered."

"I fell asleep."

"You're probably exhausted from not getting much sleep last night."

"Max said I'd only slept about thirty minutes." She'd spent a couple hours in his company, but it seemed much shorter.

"So Carl is history?" Crystal asked as she drove into town and turned toward their apartment complex. It was nice living in the same complex as your best friend.

"Yes."

"Thank God."

Sierra turned in her seat. "You didn't like him? You never said anything."

"I didn't like the way he treated you at times. He was an ass when you told him you didn't do horror, and look. He lied and took you anyway."

"Well, it's done and over with. I'm moving on."

"Good. Now move on to Max."

"Not wasting any time, are we?" She wanted to laugh but his touch sent shivers of awareness through her bloodstream.

"You'll find I get right to the point of most matters."

"You certainly do."

Max guided her from her office, and Sierra halted next to Amy's desk. "I'm leaving for the day. Go ahead and send the phones to the service and take off."

"Glad you're leaving early. You've had too many long days," Amy said.

"Long days?" Max whispered.

"I'll see you tomorrow," Sierra said to Amy. "Oh, the Pearl Group is my 9 a.m. appointment."

"I'll grab some bagels and pastries and make sure there's coffee. Go." Amy waved her hand and Max urged her toward the elevator. She usually took the stairs, but not today.

"How many long days have you had?" Max asked as the elevator descended.

"Just Saturday, and Monday." Too many even for her. While Saturday had been interesting, Monday had been filled with too many meetings.

Max kept a hold of her elbow as he escorted her out of the building. "Is Sweet and Savory good for you?"

"Oh yes. Lara's place is great." Sierra loved patronizing local businesses, and Lara had the best coffee and pastries in the area.

"I've only heard about it. I haven't been there."

"You're in for a treat." Sierra noticed Max automatically took her left side, walking closer to the curb and street. Protective male. Not that she didn't know that already. The way he cupped her elbow to guide her was another clue.

They walked into Sweet and Savory. Max chose a table for two in the back. "What would you like?" he asked.

"A vanilla latte and a piece of German chocolate cake, if she has any." Lara's cakes were to die for, and since she'd barely eaten today, it wouldn't hurt her waistline.

"Done."

Sierra watched Max stride up to the counter and place their order. A shiver went up her spine again. What was it about Max? Yes, he was imposing, a dominant male, but there was something else. She couldn't quite put her finger on it, but whatever it was, it made her insides melt. Not good if she wasn't going to let Max in her life.

A shadow crossed her face, and she turned her head. Oh, crap. "Hello, Carl." She hadn't seen him in the café.

"Don't *hello* me, Sierra." He sat down and stared at her. His gaze was frantic, and his hands shook. Oh hell, this was not good.

"Carl…" she started. Sierra was beginning to wonder if Carl was into drugs. They'd only dated for two months; it was possible he hid it from her. She needed to stay calm. The last thing she wanted was a big scene.

"You listen to me." His voice was low and tight. "I put up with your little display this weekend, but there is no reason to break up. You embarrassed me in front of my friends."

Yep, that was the other thing that had made Monday a long day. Carl had left her voicemail after voicemail trying to get her to reconsider breaking up with him. There was nothing to reconsider.

Sierra stared at him. She heard the honesty in his words, and while he was an alpha male she suspected his caveman instincts had launched into full alert when he saw her that night. Alone, wet, and in the dark.

"Just don't let it happen again. I don't need the 'Me Tarzan, you Jane' routine again."

"Noted."

Sierra admired his willingness to talk, and he wasn't one to beat around the bush. Well, neither was she. She took another bite of her cake, letting it melt on her tongue before she answered about his question about kink. "I'm not into the lifestyle. I am curious about it." It was as truthful as she could be at this point.

"Curiosity is good." He pulled out a card and slid it across the table to her. "My address with directions. Come out on Thursday evening at seven. Casual dress."

"What for?"

"Come and find out." His tone was low and seductive.

Sierra looked at the card. Wicked Sanctuary. The WS carved into the oak door Saturday night. Interesting. The name sent chills of excitement through her body. What a play on words. But exactly what did it mean? She nodded and slipped the card into her purse.

"With that taken care of, would you like to go to dinner?"

She let out a laugh. "Give the man an opening, and he pounces. I can't." Max stilled in his seat. "Honestly, I have to do very mundane things tonight like laundry and cleaning."

"Because of the long days your assistant mentioned?"

"Yes. And being gone over the weekend." She wasn't going to mention Carl's calls. She was over Carl.

Max nodded. "Very well, but I fully expect to see you Thursday night."

"What happens if I don't show up?"

"I will come after you."

His deadpan tone had her staring at him. Oh, yes, she could see it in his eyes; he would come after her. "Max…" she started. She needed to nip this in the bud.

"Sierra." He placed his hand over hers. "I apologize again. I'm falling back into that protective caveman in me. I'm not going to lie. You bring out that side of me, more so than I expected." He took a breath and squeezed her hand. "There is something between us, but I believe in consent. Totally and completely. If you don't appear on Thursday so be it. I won't stalk you or anything like that."

"I appreciate that." She did. After Carl and his crap, she needed a man who understood consent and her fears.

"Come on. I'll walk you back to your office so you can get your car." He released her hand and stood.

"How do you know I don't walk to my office?"

"I don't, but my car is in your lot."

Sierra shook her head and stood. They walked back to the lot in silence. "Which one is yours?" she asked. There were several in the lot she didn't recognize.

"Black one, over there." He pointed to a high-end luxury vehicle. "Where is yours?"

"Right here." She paused next to her small, silver SUV.

"Good vehicle for you." He stood and waited until she unlocked the doors, and he opened the driver's door for her.

"If you do not sign the non-disclosure form, you will not be allowed to stay. Ralph will escort you from the premises." Max gestured to Ralph lounging against the wall inside the room. "We take everyone's safety and privacy seriously."

"I can't." The man stood up, and Ralph followed him out.

The two couples talked among themselves, then one couple got up. "Sorry," the man said, and he escorted his wife out of the room. When no one else moved, Max nodded and picked up folders from one stack on the table.

"Fill these out fully. I will also stress that all answers must be truthful in order for you to get the most out of Wicked Sanctuary. We do not tolerate lying. If you lie on your application you will be expelled."

A folder was set down in front of each person along with a black pen. "Start with the top forms, and then we'll move on."

Sierra opened the folder; the NDA was first. She read it through, twice. It really was to protect the club members. You didn't discuss who was in the club and what the person did while there. Seemed fair enough. She signed off on it.

The background check wasn't anything new to her. She'd been required to have a background check for the non-profit job. They actually did one every year. Sierra filled the form out, then she shut the folder.

"Done already?" Max asked quietly.

"Yes."

"No qualms?"

"A million, but not about an NDA or background check."

Max smiled. "That's my girl."

Sierra glared at him and held onto the folder as he tried to take it.

He winked at her and she let go. Max took the folder and put it into a separate pile. As the others finished, he did the same thing. Another man walked into the room, and Sierra realized it was the same man who'd come into Max's office Saturday night. He picked up the folders and left.

"Now, this next set will take you a while," Max said as he passed out another folder that was much thicker. "This is your application, rules, and questionnaire. A reminder to be honest, especially with the questionnaire." He set the folder in front of her and gave her a wink. "If you need help or have questions, just ask."

Sierra opened the folder. Okay, first page, pretty standard. Name, date of birth, phone, emergency contact, gender identity, preferred pronouns. She filled those out quickly. Then she hesitated. The next set of choices: Dom, Submissive, Switch, Unsure.

Holy crap! Her guess was right. Wicked Sanctuary was a BDSM club. Her head snapped up, and her gaze met Max's. Well, that explained the book he gave her, but also a few other things. Sometimes she was a little dense. Max sauntered over to her.

"Problem?"

"Umm, no." Her hand shook.

Max leaned down. "In case you were wondering, you are a submissive."

"Not your decision to make."

"I know." He sauntered back to the front of the room.

"You wish," she whispered under her breath.

"Shoo." She motioned with her hands for him to leave.

He raised his eyebrows at her, then chuckled, and returned to the front of the room.

Forty minutes later, Sierra sat back and let out a sigh. She was only about half done, and her brain was going in circles. She needed a break. She stood up and Max was at her side.

"I need a break. Is it okay if I go out to the parking lot and get some fresh air?"

"Sure." He flipped her folder closed. "Regina." The young woman padded over from where she was lounging. "Please take Sierra out front for some fresh air, and bring her back in when she's ready."

"Yes, Sir." Regina motioned to Sierra. "If you'll come with me."

"Thank you." Sierra followed her. When Regina opened the front door, Sierra was surprised to see an almost empty parking lot. Then again, there weren't that many of them here to begin with.

She stepped outside and took a deep breath. The smell of pine and freshly mowed grass filled her senses. "Regina, may I ask you some questions?"

"Sure. I'll answer what I can."

"How long have you been a member?"

"Three years."

"Forgive me if I'm wrong, but you are a submissive?"

"Oh yes."

"Can you tell me more? I've read books, but I'd really like to hear your perspective."

Regina smiled. "It's the best thing in the world. Once I'm inside Wicked Sanctuary, I can let go of everything. My worries, my thoughts, my fears. The Dom I play with that night will take care of me and allow me to just be me without judgment."

Sierra found the idea of letting go appealing. Sometimes, when she was overwhelmed, she would put on music and lie on her bed in the dark, letting it take her away. This sounded close to the same thing. Except on a more physical level.

"You said the Dom you play with that night. You have different ones?"

"I'm what is called a club submissive. I prefer to play with different Doms. Just like us, Doms have their hard limits. Sometimes I need more than the one I usually play with can give me."

Sierra nodded. Interesting concept. Her analytical mind was thinking about this on a psychological plane. Needs and wants fulfilled. The concept wasn't as foreign as it sounded. But these were emotional needs and maybe physical as well.

"Don't you get attached to your Dom?" There were emotions involved; it would be hard not to get attached.

Regina shook her head. "Not really. I enjoy playing with some more than others, but it's more of an emotional release they can get from me."

"I'm not sure I understand." She was trying to wrap her mind around all of this.

At the last minute before leaving the club, Max grabbed Sierra's folder. The pathway lights led the way. Max unlocked the door that led into his home office, and he and Jordan made their way into the family room.

"Do you need food with the beer?" Max asked as Jordan grabbed the remote and turned on the sixty-inch TV. Max set the folder on the side table away from Jordan.

"If you have something. I didn't eat dinner."

"When don't I have something?" Max sauntered to the kitchen. He hadn't eaten either, and now his stomach was protesting. Grabbing lunchmeat out of the fridge along with condiments and beer, Max made a couple of sandwiches and then went back into the family room. "Here you go." He set the plates and beers on the coffee table.

"Thanks." Jordan picked up his plate and began eating.

Max glanced at the screen as he ate his sandwich. He liked football, but tonight, his mind was on Sierra's questionnaire. What had she put down? He was itching to find out.

"You're distracted," Jordan said.

"What?" Max placed the empty plate on the coffee table and sipped his beer to give him time to think of an answer.

"Our favorite team has scored three touchdowns in the last five minutes. You haven't even reacted. I would say a particular new sub has wormed her way into your head."

"You aren't wrong." She had. More than he thought possible.

Jordan laughed. "Then I'll take my leave so you can read her questionnaire and plan for what fun, delightful things you will do with her." Max started to protest, but Jordan waved him off. "We can talk tomorrow. Because I'll admit I'm curious about this woman as well. Not as a play partner, but because she has you tied up in knots."

Within a few minutes, Jordan was gone, and Max sat down with the folder in his lap. He opened it. She'd circled unsure instead of sub. Interesting. Then he went down the list of kink activities.

They'd talked about impact play and she'd circled she was comfortable being flogged on her butt and back; the rest were no. After her reaction to the question, he wasn't surprised. There was something in her past.

The next page was about bondage. Mainly light to medium, which was fine with him. They could move up to the heavy stuff if needed. Her noes were areas that he wasn't concerned with.

He imagined Sierra spread-eagled on his bed, her body rosy from his hand and a light flogger. The shine of her juices gleamed in the light. She would wriggle and his cock tightened as he planned what he would do to her next.

Max shook his head. *Let's not get ahead of the game.* Sierra was compatible with him in more ways than one. He continued through the list. Lots of noes, which he expected from a novice. He paused. Nipple clamps and nipple play were a yes. He bet he could make a feast out of her nipples from what he saw Saturday night.

Voluntary nudity was a yes, but forced a no. He was fine with that. He wanted his sub to be comfortable until she was ready. He kept reading until he got to the last page that talked about sex toys.

She'd forgotten about it. Then again, she'd been trying to forget about Carl. He was making that impossible.

"Yeah, Max." He was yelling now. "Bastard that took my place."

Sierra stayed still as the police walked up behind Carl. He was so high he didn't even notice.

"He didn't take your place. We were just having coffee." One of the officers nodded at her and grinned.

"Sir, you need to let go of the lady. Now," the second officer said.

Carl spun around, and Sierra cried out as he pulled her with him. The officer who had nodded at her grabbed Carl's wrist.

"He said, let her go." The voice of the officer who'd grinned at her was hard and cold. She shivered.

Carl's face turned red, then the pressure on her arm was gone. The officer dropped Carl's wrist and pulled her away.

"Damn cops," Carl yelled at them. "I'm having a conversation with my girlfriend."

"You need to calm down, sir," the second officer said.

"Fuck off." Carl lunged for her, and the officer holding her out of harm's way blocked him.

"Sir." The second officer grabbed him, and pulled his hands behind his back.

Carl wrenched his arm free and swung at the officer, missing by a wide arc. The officer next to her lunged at Carl and, within seconds, both officers had him on the ground.

"Sir, you need to calm down and stop fighting." The officer put a knee in Carl's back.

"Screw you."

The officer shook his head, and Sierra heard the click of cuffs as they were put around Carl's wrists. Together the officers hauled Carl to his feet.

"Are you okay?" the officer who got Carl to release her asked.

Was she okay? Sierra held out her hand, surprised to see it shaking. She clutched it to her chest, willing herself to calm down now. *You're safe. He's not a threat any more.*

"Yes, thank you, Officer—?"

"Wolfe, Logan Wolfe."

"Sierra Blake."

Officer Wolfe's eyes widened, then he grinned. "Sorry we're meeting under these circumstances."

Carl continued to swear and yell. Sierra winced when he called her a whore. "Bruce, do you need help getting him in the car?"

"No. He's high, but nothing I can't handle." The other officer marched her ex to the patrol car with Carl yelling and struggling the whole way.

"I'll need you to come down to the station and make a statement. I'm assuming you want to press charges." Officer Wolfe's voice was calm and soothing, which helped Sierra regain her sense of balance.

"Yes, I would." She made the decision quickly. She had to do this; otherwise, Carl would continue to bother her.

"Good. Why don't you follow us, and I can take your statement while my partner processes the assailant."

"Sounds good." She blew out a breath. So much for time to relax before class tonight.

"Hey boss, Miss Sierra." He grinned at them. "Jordan and the Websters are already in the classroom."

"Thanks, Ralph." Sierra tossed the burger wrapper in the trash, and Max led her down the hallway. "Go take a seat," he said once they were inside the classroom, then he strode up to Jordan.

"You're strung tight," Jordan remarked.

"The bastard hurt her." Max pointed to his arm, and Jordan looked over at Sierra. The reddened area on her upper arm was easy to see. "I want to beat his ass into the ground."

"Settle down. Do you want me to go first?"

"No. It's better if we do things in order. This might be a little too slow for the Websters."

"I advised them that we would be going over things they might already know, and they were fine with that."

Max nodded and took a deep breath. Jordan had set everything up already. That was a plus.

"Good evening. Since there are only three of you, the classes will be a little more informal. First off. While you're here in Wicked Sanctuary, all Doms will be addressed as Sir or Ma'am unless they tell you otherwise." He moved around to the front of the table. "We'll give you a copy of everything you signed last week, the club rules, bylaws, etc. for you to take home with you and study."

He glanced over at Sierra, who sat staring at him. Her eyes were bright, but her attention was on him. Good. He went over everything he wanted to cover, then Jordan stepped forward and told them, next Saturday night, they would experience the club for the first time as new members.

When the session ended, Max joined Sierra, folder in hand. "Everything good? You looked confused at times." She hadn't asked any questions, but at times, her eyes clouded with doubt.

"Ummm… I have some questions, but kind of feel a little stupid." Her cheeks turned pink.

"I see. There is no stupid question, only an unasked one. So talk to me."

"How does one know if one is dominant or submissive?"

He almost laughed, but he could see she was serious. How could he answer that one? He looked over at the sofa grouping that had been moved into the classroom area in prep for tomorrow night's private party. "Come with me." He held out his hand, and she took it.

He sat and then pulled her down into his lap.

"Max." She squirmed. His cock twitched. *Down boy.*

"Be still and listen to me."

She froze and tilted her head back to look up at him.

"I'm going to ask you a few questions, I'll give you choices, and you give me your gut reaction."

"Okay."

"During sex, do you like to be on top? Yes or no."

She tilted her head. "Sometimes."

He shook his head. "That wasn't a choice, but I'll take it. Being pulled into my arms and told to be still, did you like it or dislike it?"

"Both." She wrinkled her nose. "Your tone startled me, but I liked how you took charge."

Oh, yes, she was submissive, but she didn't quite see it yet. "Do you like the idea of being tied up during sex? Yes, no, or unsure."

Color flooded her cheeks. "Yes," she whispered.

"Sierra." He gave her a sexy look and dang if a shiver of excitement didn't shoot down her spine.

"What can I do for you?" She unlocked her vehicle and threw her purse in.

"I'd like to take you to dinner."

Sierra tilted her head and stared at him. "You couldn't call?"

"I wanted to surprise you."

"That you did." Why did her nipples tighten at his words? "We just saw each other last night."

"Yes, but I thought it would be good for us to see each other outside the club." He leaned over. "Especially if we're going to have any sort of relationship."

Sierra ducked her head as heat filled her cheeks. "I bet no woman ever refuses you." She looked at him from beneath her lashes.

"You have no idea." A grin played around his lips. "Dinner?"

At least he was asking her and not ordering her to have dinner with him. "Why not? Where shall I meet you?" While she'd been alone with Max before, having her own car would make things easier. She didn't like leaving her car in the office lot.

He cocked his head as if considering her question. "Don't you trust me?"

She did, but...what? If he was going to take advantage of her, he would have done it long before now, especially the way they'd met. "I do. I need to take my car home."

He gave her a grin. "I'll follow you, and then we'll go to dinner."

She nodded. It was a good compromise.

An hour later, they were seated in a back booth at the local bar and grill. Sierra took in the laid-back decor. She hadn't been in the bar and grill before. Wood paneling, bright lights and several television screens around the restaurant made sports-watching easy. The bar stood in the middle with the restaurant built around it.

This was just what she needed, a place where she could chill out with some good food and good company. They ordered, and then Max turned to her.

"Am I allowed to ask questions about the club?" she said.

"Of course."

"Good. Why did you decide to open the club?"

"Jordan, Damon and I came up with the idea of our own club."

"I met Jordan Saturday night and again in the classroom, right?"

"Yes, you haven't met Damon yet. The three of us met at a munch."

"Munch? That's a meeting of like-minded people in the lifestyle."

"I see you've been reading."

"I have." She'd read several of the books from the list he'd given her.

"And?"

"And what? You promised to tell me about how you started the club." She stared at him. Sierra really wanted to know more about the club.

"Dog with a bone." He smiled at her.

Damn that smile made her insides melt. She hadn't been like this with any other man. "I really want to know. So you all attended a munch together."

"Yes. One night, we got to talking about how some of the private parties just weren't doing it for us, and how it would be nice to go somewhere to play without worrying about noise or there not being enough room."

"Private parties at someone's home?" Somehow that didn't seem safe to her.

"Most of the time yes."

"So why weren't they working?"

"There are many levels of BDSM, some more hardcore than others."

Sierra nodded. "Like sadism." A small shiver slid up her spine. The waitress delivered their food and left. The smell of her hamburger made her stomach growl. "Please continue," she said, grabbing a french fry.

"Sadism and other things, but a lot of our concern was that the parties were becoming nothing more than nightly hookups for some people. We wanted not only to play, but to educate, to allow people to explore their kinks without boundaries, if possible."

"There are things you don't allow at the club?" She picked up her burger and took a bite.

"Yes, due to health concerns for some, and others because we felt they are too unsafe." He took a bite of his beef dip sandwich.

"Like breath play."

His eyes widened. "Correct. What do you know about breath play?"

Heat filled her face. "I came across it in some of the reading I've done." She didn't have to tell him that in the last romance she read there was breath play in the book. While it seemed more intimate than intercourse, it had scared her, and she almost hadn't finished the book. She'd told Tessa to tone down the books. She couldn't read another one like that.

"Reading is different than experiencing."

Wasn't that the truth? Sierra reached out and picked up her water glass when her throat tightened. It was as if her father's hands were on her neck, squeezing. She took a sip of water, trying to ease the pressure.

"You've gone pale. What is it?"

The concern in his voice brought her back to the present. She took a deep breath and another sip of water and pushed away the memories. "It's nothing. So how did the club happen?"

He frowned, and the hard look in his eyes told her he was only letting this go right now for her sake.

"My family has always owned land in Pleasant Valley, so building it here was easy for me since I had the land and I could build the club."

"That must have taken a lot of capital."

"It did." He shifted. "I made money in IT and from my video games."

"I knew it. Computer geek."

He stared at her then laughed. "I don't like the word 'geek', but coming from you, it sounds sexy." He touched her nose with his finger. "How did you come to work with the non-profit?"

"Deflecting the conversation." She let out a small sigh. "When I was a teenager, a neighbor tried to kill his family. Her daughter was my friend. My friend was distraught and there seemed to be no one to help her."

"How long ago was this?"

"About seventeen years ago, when I was fifteen. They sent my friend to a counselor, but he didn't help; in fact, he made her worse. She would come to my house, sit in my room, and we would talk for hours."

"She needed a friend."

"Yes, but she needed some emotional help too. Something, as her friend, I wasn't qualified to give. I found a non-profit group to help her, and I realized they did really good work."

"And your kink knowledge?"

"College." Her fingers tangled together in her lap. "My boyfriend and I experimented."

"Tell me more."

"Boring stuff really. I was getting my degree in economics and psychology, and a guest lecturer in one of the many psychology classes I took talked about kink and kink-friendly doctors. Many of the students made jokes, others just stayed quiet."

"I bet you were a quiet one."

"Got you fooled." She laughed. "I actually told people to shut up. I wanted to hear what he had to say. When the lecture was over, many of my fellow students thought the lecture was crap."

"Idiots."

"They were, mainly because they ignored what was said, and when it came up during the final, they couldn't answer the questions." She'd been proud of herself for not shutting down during the lecture, even when some of it made her uncomfortable.

"Bet you could."

"Yep." Pride filled her. Others dismissed her knowledge, but not Max. He seemed to like that she studied and listened. He made her feel worthy.

"So tell me..."

His cell rang. He looked at the screen. "I'm sorry. I have to take this."

"It's fine. Do you need to go outside?"

He hated being interrupted just as he got her talking. "No. It should only take a minute."

Max put his cell to his ear. "Preston here."

"Max, Jordan, sorry to bug you but we need you at the club ASAP."

Max let out a groan. "I left you in charge, Jordan." They had a private party going on tonight.

"I know." Jordan's voice lowered. "I'm really sorry. We've got a major issue. One that I need you here as the owner. I've already taken care of separating the parties involved, but Mr. Cook is insisting on talking with you."

Max fought against swearing. "All right. Be there in twenty." He hit *end* and looked at Sierra. She was people-watching, trying to give him some privacy. "I'm sorry, but I need to cut this short."

"I understand. You do have a business to run." She slid out of the booth and stood. At least they'd finished eating.

Max motioned to the waitress and handed her money to cover their meal and a tip, and led Sierra out his vehicle. He helped her up into his big SUV.

"Do you want to drop me off first? Or go straight to the club?" she asked when he started the SUV.

Her question made him stop and think. "The club, if you don't mind. It's a private party, and something's apparently happened."

"I don't mind."

Max drove fast, but not so fast that it wasn't safe. Several things ran through his mind at once. While Cook was a good man, Max didn't like some of the people he brought in for private parties. It figured that the one night he took off, there would be issues.

The parking lot of the club was full. Max frowned. There shouldn't be this many cars. He parked and looked at Sierra. "Do you want to wait here or inside?"

She glanced out at the dark night. "Inside, please."

He nodded. Hopefully, he could take care of this quickly and they could continue their night. Max pushed open the door to the club. He could hear the shouting out in reception.

Ralph wasn't at the desk. This was not good. "Wait here behind the desk." If there was a fight or worse, he wanted her out of the line of fire. She glared at him for a moment, but she stepped behind the desk. "Yes, Sir."

Max barely fought against grinning. Spunky sub. He gave her a quick, hard kiss, then headed through the doors to the club proper.

Jordan and Cook were facing off, while Damon and Ralph held two men back that Max didn't know. Others stood watching like it was a movie or something. Max strode over to Jordan and Cook. "What the hell is going on?"

"Good, you're here." Cook stepped away from Jordan. "This one doesn't understand how my parties work."

Jordan stiffened.

"Jordan knows exactly what your parties are like, and what I don't allow in my club. What rules were violated?" It had to be something serious for Jordan to call him.

"Alcohol, drugs, and non-consent," Jordan bit out.

"He overreacted," Cook said.

"Are you saying your people didn't bring alcohol and drugs in here?" Max crossed his arms over his chest. He could see the beer bottles on the tables, and if he wasn't mistaken, Cook smelled of weed, and there was some fine white powder on one of the tables.

"Well..."

"Don't give me any bullshit, I have eyes. I warned you last time this happened. One more time would be your last."

"Come on Max, you can't mean—"

A scream cut off Cook. Max stiffened, and his gut clenched. He knew instantly who it was. He turned and ran for the reception area.

****

Waiting behind the desk like Max had told her, Sierra was focused on the voices, trying to hear what was going on, so she didn't see the man until he was in front of her.

"Well, aren't you a pretty thing."

The man's face was flushed, his pupils dilated.

Shit. "I'm with Max." That should scare him away. She hoped.

"Here to play." He moved toward her, the leer in his voice sending tendrils of fear up her spine.

"No." She threw some authority behind her voice, but he kept advancing.

Oh crap. She looked around for a weapon. Her eyes fell on the stapler, but before she could reach for it, the man grabbed her arm where Carl had grabbed her last night.

"Let go," she said, wincing.

"Want to play." His words were slurred.

She opened her mouth to scream, and he placed his beefy hand over her mouth and part of her nose, cutting off her air. Instant panic hit Sierra. Without thinking, she slammed her knee up between his legs. The man roared and let go.

Sierra drew in a deep breath and screamed *red* at the top of her lungs.

Max came flying down the hallway with Jordan, Ralph, and two men she didn't know following. "Sierra." His voice filled with emotion, Max put his body between her and the man who'd grabbed her. "Are you okay?"

She nodded. She was okay now that he was here. Sierra was pleased with herself for defending herself even in the midst of her panic. Memories flooded her mind, and she fought to push them away.

"I just wanted to play," the man wheezed.

"Shut up." Max's voice was hard and cold. "Sierra?"

"I'm okay." Her voice was shaking, damn it.

Max's fist clenched. She started to reach for him when another man spoke.

"No harm, no—"

"I don't want to hear one more word from you, Cook." Max whirled around and faced the man. "Out. Everyone out now. And you, Cook"—he stabbed a finger at Cook—"are no longer welcome here. None of you are. I'll be sending you a bill for damages."

Needing to feel more in control, Sierra angled her head so she could see around Max.

"If you don't pay it, it will be my pleasure to sue your ass," Jordan said.

The man dressed in leather pants shook his head. "I'll get everyone out."

"We'll help," the other man said and motioned to Jordan and Ralph, then he looked at the man who tried to assault her. "But first let me get this piece of trash out." He grabbed him by the back of the neck and pushed him to the door and then out, before slamming it shut.

"Trash removed. Take care of her."

"Thanks, Damon," Max said, and he turned to Sierra. "Let me take you into my office." He slipped his arm around her shoulders, tucking her close to his body.

She appreciated his warmth and strength, since she couldn't seem to stop shaking. As they walked, she pushed the memories of her childhood back into the box and fought to put the lid back on it. Max guided her into his office and onto the sofa.

He knelt down and framed her face with his palms. "I don't want to leave you, but I need to go help."

"It's okay," she whispered. Max closed his eyes but not before she saw the worry there. Her stomach tightened. He was worried about her. Warmth filled her veins. "I'll be fine, Max." She reached up, willing her hand to not shake as she ran her fingers over his face. This man was always catching her at her worst. A drowned cat, Carl, and now this guy. Would she and Max ever have a normal night together?

"Ralph will be guarding the door. No one will come in but me." He leaned forward and brushed a kiss over her lips before standing. At the door, he glanced back at her, and she gave him a nod.

The door shut quietly behind him, and Sierra collapsed against the sofa. She needed to get her emotions under control before Max came back.

****

Anger flowed through Max like lava. Oh yes, he was a volcano ready to explode.

"Ralph," Max yelled as he stood in the doorway of the club.

"Yes, boss," Ralph said, jogging over to him.

"Guard my office. No one but me goes in."

"You got it." Ralph headed to the office where Sierra waited, and Max looked around.

He shook his head. What a mess. Tables were littered with bottles and lord knew what else. He watched Jordan and Damon usher the rest of the group out. Cook stood off to one side. Max approached him.

"I'm sorry, Max. I didn't realize it was this bad," Cook said.

Max stared at Cook. "Your group, your responsibility." He wasn't going to back down. Cook knew the rules and had been warned the last time.

"I know." Cook let out a sigh.

A young lady came up to them. The woman's face was streaked with tears. "I can't go with him. I can't."

Max's senses went on alert. There was something in her voice.

"Now, Jackie," Cook started.

Max raised his hand. "What seems to be the problem?" He kept his tone even to avoid scaring the woman more.

"I can take care of this," Cook said.

"My club." Max glared at him before turning his attention back to the woman. "Jackie, is it?"

"Yes, Sir."

"Why don't we go sit over there"—he waved to one of the clean tables—"and you can tell me what's going on."

"Now see here—" Cook started again.

"Damon," Max called.

"What's up?" Damon asked.

"Escort Cook out while I talk with this young lady."

"With pleasure." Damon took Cook by the arm and pulled him toward the door while Cook continued to complain.

"Shall we?" Max gestured to the chairs.

"Thank you, Sir." She padded over to the chairs.

Max grabbed a couple of napkins and handed them to her as he sat down. "What has you so upset?" The woman's eyes lowered, and Max sighed. "I know you don't know me, but I own this club. Whatever you tell me is between us. I only want to help you."

Jackie wiped her tears. "I came in with some friends. One of them was going to be my Dom for the evening."

"Okay, but you said you couldn't go with him. Who is the him? Cook?"

"No. He..." Fresh tears welled. "I'm the one who went to Master Jordan with the report of non-consent. The 'him' is the Dom I was going to play with." She sniffled. "He wanted me to do things that are hard limits for me and tried to force the issue. I don't have a ride home, and I'm afraid to go with him and my friends."

Max bit back a curse. "I see. I can have someone take you home, so you don't have to ride with your friends."

"It's not only that." Her voice shook. "He knows where I live."

He got it now. "Can you give me a few minutes? I think I might have a solution."

"Thank you, Sir."

Max wanted to tell her to stop with the sir, but decided not to. After all, they were still in the club. He moved across the room and pulled out his cell phone. "Hey Colby, this is Max. Sorry to bug you. Any chance I could borrow a couple of your biker friends for tonight?"

"Sure Max, how many you need?"

"Two should do it."

"Fine. What should I tell them?"

"I've got a sub whose non-consent rights were almost violated, and she's afraid he'll come after her at home."

"Bastard. I'll have them at the club parking lot in fifteen."

"Thanks." Max hung up and walked back over to Jackie. "Jackie." Her head rose, her eyes red and puffy. "I've got some friends coming. I don't want you to be afraid; they are biker friends. They'll take you home and stay outside your house to protect you."

"Oh, thank you, Sir." She started to reach for him then pulled back.

He appreciated that she understood and followed rules. No touching without permission. "Permission to hug granted."

She jumped up and gave him a tight hug before stepping back. "I didn't know what to do."

"If you need the bikers to stay longer than just tonight, let them know in the morning, and they'll make sure someone else comes. They can watch out for you as long as you need." She opened her mouth. "No more thank yous. Now, why don't you go wash your face before my friends get here?"

"Yes, Sir." She hurried out of the room, and Max followed. Damon and Jordan waited for him.

"All gone except for the young woman who ran into the bathroom just now," Jordan said.

"Jackie. She'll be gone in a few. Colby is sending some friends over to take her home and watch over her tonight."

Jordan's jaw tightened. They all believed in consent above anything else. Violate that and you got what you deserved. "Good."

"What about the mess in there?" Damon asked, gesturing toward the club.

"I'll call the cleaning crew and have them come out tomorrow. Cook is going to get one hell of a bill for all of this." Max ran his hand over his head.

"He should," Jordan said as Jackie came out of the bathroom. She approached the men slowly, almost tentatively.

The roar of bikes could be heard. "That's your ride." He looked at the young lady. "Damn, you can't ride a bike like that." She had on a short, short dress.

"I've got something." Damon ran into the men's room and came back out with a pair of sweats and sweatshirt. "They're clean. They will be big, but it's the best I can do for now."

He handed the clothes to Jackie and she slipped them on. The three of them walked Jackie outside to where the two bikers waited. Max shook their hands and introduced Jackie to them, then explained a bit of what had happened.

Jackie gave them her address. One of the bikers helped her onto the back of his bike, the other gave her a helmet before he got on his bike and they took off.

Max, Jordan, and Damon walked back inside the club. Ralph still stood outside Max's office.

"We'll lock up. Why don't you go take care of Sierra," Jordan said.

"Thanks." Max made his way to his office. "Go home, Ralph, and thanks for your help tonight."

"Anytime boss. If you need me early for anything tomorrow, give me a call." Ralph left.

Max opened the door and walked into his office. Sierra sat deathly still on the sofa, staring off into space. Not good.

"Sierra, honey." No response. He didn't want to frighten her.

"Sierra," he said louder.

Her head snapped to the side. Her eyes were unfocused. "Oh, hi, Max."

Damn, he shouldn't have left her alone. "Come on, honey. Let's get you out of here." They made it out to his SUV in record time, and he drove out of the club driveway and into the one next door.

"Where are you taking me?"

"My house."

Chapter Seven

"I don't think that's a good idea," Sierra said as he drove down the driveway to his home.

"I do." He reached over and took her hand in his. "You don't need to be alone tonight."

She shook her head. "I want to go home, Max." Her voice was soft.

"Will you be alone if I take you home?"

"Yes." Her hand trembled in his.

Max's protective instincts went on high alert. The last time he left a sub alone, she... No, he wouldn't think about that. He wouldn't allow it to happen this time.

"Sierra." Her hand jerked in his at his hard tone. Well, she better get used to it. He'd used his Dom voice, and tonight, she was going to listen. "You've had a trauma tonight. I'll take you home if that's what you really want, but in good conscience, I can't leave you alone."

He glanced over at her. Her lips were pressed together, while her other hand clenched the door rest.

"Always the alpha male," she said.

Max would have laughed if this hadn't been so serious. Tension radiated off her in waves. His Sierra was a strong woman, but she'd been assaulted twice in forty-eight hours. He feared she was going to break, and he wanted to be there when she did.

He stopped his vehicle at the gate. "What's your decision?"

Her gaze clashed with his, and she let out a sigh. "I'll stay." Max wanted to do a victory yell, but he had a feeling there would be more battles between them.

"You have a gate here too?" There was curiosity in her voice.

"Yes. More privacy." He hit the remote, and the gate opened. "There's a call box, plus friends have a code to use."

"You're big on privacy."

"That I am." Mainly because he had a bitch of an ex-wife, and he didn't want any surprises. That is, if she ever found out he lived here. When they were married, they had a house in town at her insistence. She'd gotten the house in the divorce and then promptly sold it. Max pulled around the driveway and heard Sierra's gasp.

His lips twitched. Being an IT guy, Max had made his home a smart home years ago. The interior lights were programmed to come on at sunset. He'd made sure the exterior lights had been set up to come on when it got dark. The blinds on the windows were also on timers and set to close later in the evening. Light spilled out onto the driveway and the walkway from the garage.

He parked his car and then made his way to Sierra's door and opened it.

"No funny business tonight. I am a bit tired."

"Noted." Max grasped her by the waist and lifted her out of his SUV, keeping his arm around her waist, and led her out of the garage and up the stone walkway.

"I'm not going to sleep with you," she said.

"I know. That's not what this night is about. I promise I won't jump your bones." Tomorrow would be another story, but he'd cross that bridge when he got to it.

"That's a lot of glass," she said, motioning to the side of the house.

"Yes. Wait until you see the rest of the house." He loved having a lot of light in his home, so all the rooms had big windows. Right now, the ones she saw were to the dining room and kitchen.

He opened the front door and guided Sierra in. He took her purse and set it on the side table, before ushering her to the family room.

"I'll give you the grand tour tomorrow."

"You're assuming I'll be here long enough tomorrow." She paused to look at him. "You've been awfully insistent I stay. Why?"

This wasn't something he wanted to get into tonight, but she was right that she deserved an answer. "I'll give you the short version. Several years ago, a sub at the club had an incident like tonight. She said she was fine and went home. She was dead the next day."

"Oh, my goodness." Her fingers caressed his cheek.

"It devastated several of us knowing we could have helped but didn't."

"How could you? She said she was fine and went home. There was no way you or anyone else could have know she was going to die."

Her compassion lifted his bruised heart. "My head knows that, but the heart thinks differently." When had he ever opened up to a woman like this? Never. "Let me take care of you tonight." He led her to the sofa and waited until she sat down. "What would you like to drink?"

Changing the subject.

"Surprise me."

Max made his way over the small bar, pulled down a glass, and poured some brandy into it, then found the orange juice in the small fridge and added it before rejoining Sierra.

"Try this."

Sierra took it and swallowed a healthy swig before setting the glass down on the side table. "Thank you."

Then she burst into tears.

Max sank down next to her on the sofa and pulled her into his arms. He'd been waiting for this. He cradled her close as she cried. After a while, her sobs turned to soft hiccups.

"I'm sorry," she whispered.

"There's no reason to be sorry. You were assaulted. I'm sorry that happened to you, especially on my turf." Max stretched out his arm and grabbed a box of tissues. He kept his arm around her while she took several and wiped her face.

"I didn't fall apart after Carl attacked me."

"You are such a strong woman, Sierra. It was bound to hit you sooner or later. I guessed sooner because of what happened tonight. I was right."

"I've gotten you all wet." She pressed a tissue against his shirt.

"That has got to be the biggest catastrophe of the night." He couldn't keep the humor from his voice. This woman constantly surprised him.

Sierra tilted her head back and gave him a small smile. "Silly man."

"Finish your drink, and I'll go find you something to wear to bed." He'd rather have her naked in his bed, but he wouldn't push her. Not yet.

"I really should go home."

"Why?" He wanted to know why going home was important to her. When she didn't answer he continued. "As I said before, let me take care of you tonight. Tomorrow you can go back to being the independent woman I know you are. There's no shame in letting someone else take the reins for a while."

"All right." She let out a sigh. "But don't think I'm going to give in this easily all the time."

"If this was easy, I don't want to see hard." He touched her nose, before standing. "Be right back."

Sierra sat back on the buttery soft light brown leather sofa and sipped her drink. She'd broken down in front of Max, and he hadn't gone running in the other direction, a new experience for her. She'd learned at an early age to hide her tears.

Max was so different. He wasn't afraid of her tears. And better yet, he understood. Sierra took in the room around her. The bar sat in one corner; across from her was a huge TV, and the couch had nice side tables. Two smaller sofas balanced out the seating.

A beautiful beige, brown, and burgundy area rug covered the dark hardwood. She turned her head and was mildly surprised to see beige drapes covering what looked like a large doorway. Interesting. She turned and looked behind her.

A small gasp left her lips. Another window wall, which revealed a patio and garden area. And was that a pool? She rose and went over to the windows. Oh yes, that was a pool. The underwater lighting reflected off the blue water.

Trees surrounded the pool deck and patio area. She loved the way ground lighting was used to illuminate the area. Moonlight shone between the tree branches in bursts. It all looked so beautiful and tranquil. Sierra set her empty glass down and moved to the French doors, opened them, and stepped outside. The night air was cool against her skin, but she didn't care.

A sense of peace soothed her senses. It was so quiet. She could hear the crickets chirping and the rustle of the trees in the slight breeze. This was heaven. No street noise, loud music, sirens.

"Are you okay?" Max asked, coming up behind her.

"Fine." She turned to him. "Your home is beautiful…and so quiet."

"Yes. But it's cool out. Tomorrow you can investigate to your heart's content." He took her by the elbow and led her back inside. Max closed the doors and locked them before leading Sierra down the hallway.

Near the dining room, he turned left. Sierra stopped in a doorway. "Holy crap! This is one hell of a bedroom." She could barely believe what she was seeing.

Max let out a chuckle. "I like it."

"I could live in this room," she muttered. A king-size bed stood off to her left. In front of her, a small sitting area, two dressers, and another doorway, which she assumed led into the master bath.

She was surprised at the neutral decor. The carpet was dark beige, with some red highlights. The comforter on the bed had a woven pattern of burgundy and dark purple. The shutters on the windows were closed. Comfort and warmth embraced her.

"I put a t-shirt and a pair of shorts in the bathroom for you. Go change." He nudged her toward the doorway and closed the door gently behind her.

Dazed, Sierra made her way into the bathroom and let out a groan. Now this was a bathroom. Double sinks, a walk-in shower with multiple water heads, including a rain shower system. The jetted tub was separate and big enough to hold several people. The walnut parquet tile complimented the light tan walls with white trim. She turned toward the mirror and almost let out a scream.

"So much for waterproof mascara." She had raccoon eyes; her hair was a mess, and her blouse was disheveled. Max had set a washcloth and towel beside the sink, along with a toothbrush and toothpaste. The man thought of everything.

She looked longingly at the shower. While she was sure Max wouldn't mind, she didn't know how she felt about getting naked with him in the other room. For tonight, she'd wash up quickly, and change. The shorts he left her had a drawstring so she could tighten them around her waist. She wasn't skinny by any means, but it did make her feel good that she needed the drawstring to keep them up.

The t-shirt was plain white and soft to the touch. Sierra hated sleeping with her bra on, so she took it off, put the t-shirt on, and looked down. Oh yeah, the girls were their normal perky selves.

She folded her clothes and set them on an empty shelf. Sierra crossed her arms over her chest and walked out of the bathroom.

Max stood near the bed. He'd turned down the covers and all the lights were off except for a small lamp by the bed. He'd changed into a pair of what looked like yoga pants.

"Come to bed, Sierra." He motioned toward the mattress.

She padded over to the bed, opposite Max, and slipped between the covers. When Max climbed in she sat up. She'd told him she wasn't going to sleep with him and she meant it. Still a twinge of regret shot through her.

"Wait a second, we're both sleeping here?"

"Yes." He reached over and turned the lamp off plunging them into darkness.

"I told you I won't have sex with you."

"I know; we're just going to sleep."

It took a few minutes for her eyes to adjust. "Don't you have another bedroom I can sleep in?"

"I do." He tugged her down to him with a gentle touch. "But I don't plan on leaving you alone tonight, so we might as well be comfortable."

"Max, you ignored me when I told you I wanted to go home, and I let you talk me into staying. We are not going to sleep together, but now you're getting into bed with me. I don't think so."

"Please be quiet." He dropped his voice down, and any further objection dried up in her throat. "You just spent twenty minutes crying, and the trauma of tonight wasn't just because of that man. Your ex-boyfriend's actions have been on your mind too. Now, close your eyes and go to sleep while I keep you safe in my arms."

He wasn't wrong. But that didn't mean she had to like it.

"All right, but again, tomorrow, I won't be this easy."

"Nothing with you has been easy," he muttered.

Sierra's lips curved up as she laid her head on his shoulder. She wasn't going to complain. This was nice, being held by Max. No one had taken care of her in a long time; it was hard for her to let go. She did feel safe with him. Her eyes closed on that thought.

****

Max's muscles relaxed as Sierra's breathing changed. She'd fallen asleep easily. She'd been through the wringer tonight, and it felt good, just holding her, knowing she was safe.

He'd fought his body's reaction to seeing her in his t-shirt and shorts. She'd crossed her arms over her chest, and he'd hidden a smile at the gesture. The t-shirt didn't hide her large breasts or the fact that her nipples were hard. Heck, he'd fought the way his dick wanted to swell.

He used his free hand, reached down and adjusted his wanton cock. The last thing she needed was to feel his boner. His tough little Sierra. Tough on the outside but gooey on the inside. He'd watched her tonight. She had strength. Max couldn't wait to get her whole story. He had a feeling she'd been taking care of herself for a long time. That was probably why she couldn't circle submissive, though she was not a dominant.

In her job maybe, and certain other aspects of her life. But even her job was serving other people. That didn't mean she was submissive. Lots of people had a job like hers. But there were little things.

Even though she argued with him about coming to his home tonight, he'd waited for the emphatic *no*, but she hadn't said it. Oh, he had used his Dom voice, the one that made the subs in the club pay close attention. That tone hadn't even phased Sierra. Although she'd stopped protesting, he hadn't expected her to give in like she had. Maybe the events of the last two nights had worn her down so much that she let him have his way.

She shifted and let out a little moan. "Shhhh, you're safe, sweetheart," he said softly, tightening his arm around her. She settled instantly. Good.

It was a while before Max closed his eyes.

A small cry brought him out of his sleep. "No please, Daddy. I'll be quiet." Her voice was soft, tiny. He shifted, cradling her close and brushing hair from her face. Her eyes were still closed, so apparently, she was dreaming.

"I promise to be good. Please don't get the strap." Now her voice was filled with emotion. Damn, she was reliving something from her childhood. He wanted to wake her but didn't want to scare her.

"Sierra, sweetheart." He kept his voice low and soft.

She squirmed in his hold. "No." She started to fight.

Max relaxed his hold on her, staying close so she wouldn't hurt herself. Damn, what should he do? He almost laughed. The big bad Dom didn't have a clue how to handle this situation.

When she started kicking, he pulled the covers off her and tried again. "Sierra, it's Max. Wake up. You're having a nightmare."

"Need to hide so he doesn't find me," she whispered.

"I'll find you a place to hide," he kept his voice soft. "Can you feel me take your hand?" He curled his hand around hers.

"Yes. Are you my angel?" Her voice had a childish quality to it.

"Tonight I am." She was caught up in her dream. "Come on. Follow me. We're going to sneak out this door, and I'll take you someplace safe." He moved her arm like they were walking. "Here we are."

"Where are we?"

"A safe place. Come sit on the grass. There. See the trees, and the fairies flittering from tree to tree." He was making this up as he went along, hoping it would help.

"So pretty. So peaceful."

Peaceful. Odd word for a child to use. Max slipped his arm around her shoulder once again, pulling her against him. "Rest up, my Sierra. I'll protect you. He won't be able to hurt you here."

She snuggled closer to him. "You smell nice. Thank you." Her body went lax against his.

Max blew out a breath. Crisis averted. Based on what he heard, he'd have to take her slowly through any type of impact play. She probably didn't even realize she had a hidden trigger.

What other things could he trigger? Is that what happened earlier at the club? All she told him was that the guy grabbed her. Could her father have done something worse? The thought sent a cold chill through him. He would tread carefully, because the last thing he wanted to do was hurt Sierra.

* * * *

95

Sierra woke the next morning wrapped in a cocoon of warmth and security. How long had it been since she had truly felt as safe as she did right now? *Never,* came the immediate answer. Oh, there had been times when she'd thought she was safe, then a nightmare would pull that rug out from underneath her.

She hated those damn nightmares. Childhood trauma. Yeah, she'd dealt with all of that during college, but it didn't stop them from destroying her nights. They weren't as frequent now, but between Carl and the club guy, seeing them both high and drunk had set her off.

Sierra didn't remember the nightmare from last night, but she knew she'd had one. She'd felt her pounding heart in the middle of the night, but had been unable to wake herself. But last night had been different. This time, there was someone else. Someone who led her to safety and protected her.

Her lashes rose. Max.

Heat flashed over her face. She was in bed with Max, cradled against his body, and he was watching her with those all-knowing hazel eyes of his.

"Good morning," he said.

"Morning," she mumbled. She probably had morning breath, and her hair was probably all over the place because it always came loose in the night. But most of all, she was in bed with him.

She wriggled in his hold. "I need to use the bathroom."

He released his hold on her, and she slipped from the bed and all but ran into the bathroom. She used the facilities, brushed her teeth, and finger combed her hair into some order and secured it at her neck. She didn't look too bad this morning, according to the mirror.

Max was hovering next to the bathroom door when she emerged. "Sorry, did I take too long?"

"No." He cupped her chin. "I've been wanting to do this all night." He lowered his head and their lips met.

Chapter Eight

Max's lips were firm against hers. Her hands flattened against his chest, as his hands slid to her back. His tongue traced the seam of her lips, looking for an entrance. She parted her lips. No fear or apprehension. She wanted him.

Damn, if this man's kisses weren't as smooth as the finest chocolate she'd ever eaten. Her fingers ran over his hard chest to his neck. Their tongues tangled, and she let out a small moan.

She'd gone from warm to boiling hot in seconds and all because of the man kissing her. Yes, she was attracted to him, but it was more than that. He'd held her last night, chased away her demons, and was now kissing her like there was no tomorrow.

"You taste of mint," he murmured when he broke the kiss.

"I couldn't kiss you with morning breath."

"Why not? I have it too."

"Oh?"

Their lips met again. Nothing was held back, tongues danced and dueled as hands caressed each other's backs.

His hand slipped down and he gripped her ass, pulling her against him. Her pelvis tightened. He was hard and her body reacted to it. She squirmed, needing to get closer to him.

"You're so fucking responsive," he muttered as their lips parted.

"I..." Heat crawled up her face. What was she doing? She started to pull away. When had she become so wanton?

"Stop." His tone was terse. "Don't pull away from me."

She froze at the tone of his voice and gazed up at him. His eyes were filled with passion and something else; she wasn't sure what it was. "Max, we shouldn't."

"We're just kissing."

She let out a harsh laugh. "I'm practically climbing on top of you, and we barely know each other."

"If you noticed, I wasn't stopping you." He rubbed his nose against hers. "I think we know more about each other than you think. There is a simple remedy. Spend the day with me and we can get to know each other."

She was tempted to say yes. So very tempted. "Maybe over breakfast we can talk." That's all she would commit to, at the moment. This was new for her. This instant attraction, lust, whatever label one wanted to put on it.

"I can do that." He brushed his lips over hers once again. "Let's go to the kitchen and see what trouble we can get into." He released all but her hand and led her to the kitchen.

"Damn, Max. Your house is a showcase," she said when they entered the kitchen.

"It's just a house." He walked over to the double-wide refrigerator.

"Seriously." She waved her hands. "Your kitchen is huge." There were stainless steel appliances and a big counter top in the middle of the room, with a four-burner cooktop set into it. She turned and discovered another stove, this one with eight burners of varying sizes and two ovens, a dishwasher, and of course, the double-wide fridge where he stood.

Counters ran all along the room, except for the bank of windows where a small table sat with a view of the trees and a courtyard.

"What would you like? Eggs, bacon, ham? French toast? Waffles? Pancakes?"

"What?" Sierra turned her gaze from the view back to Max.

"Breakfast, Sierra. Concentrate."

"It depends. Am I cooking?"

Max turned and frowned at her. "Absolutely not. You are my guest. I'll cook."

Why did him cooking for her make her heart skip beats? Maybe because none of the men she'd ever dated thought about cooking her breakfast. They always expected her to do it.

"Chef's choice."

"You got it. Have a seat." He gestured to the breakfast bar.

"I can help. Would you like me to get coffee started?" She could use some caffeine.

"Sure. If you open that cabinet over there on that counter top." He pointed to the one next to the archway to the dining room. "Lift the roll top part of the cabinet, you'll see the coffee machine and pods. Pick a flavor and make a pot, I'm not picky."

Sierra padded over to the area, and opened the roll-top cabinet to see a gleaming pot and a carousel with coffee pods. She picked one of her favorite breakfast blends, filled the reservoir with water and hit the *on* button.

"Mugs?"

"Cabinet to your right." He motioned with his chin as he mixed up eggs in a bowl.

She pulled down two mugs and then leaned against the cabinet, watching him. He separated the bacon, and put it in the pan, then added some ham as well. "I hope scrambled eggs are all right."

"Perfect." She was enjoying herself, watching him cook. His chest muscles did their own little dance as he moved and cooked. Soon the kitchen was filled with the scents of cooking bacon and coffee. Sierra couldn't help smiling; this felt right, comfortable even.

She poured them both a full mug and took them to the breakfast bar. "How do you take your coffee?"

"Black. There's creamer in the fridge, and sugar in the cabinet next to the sink if you need it."

Sierra got the creamer, and brought it over to the breakfast bar. "Plates?"

"Cabinet next to the mugs, silverware in the drawer below."

She retrieved everything and set them up. It was fun working with him in the kitchen. She could get used to this.

Sierra froze in place. She was comfortable with Max, and that was a first for her with a man. Usually she hated being in a kitchen with a guy.

"I'm not sure what you're thinking, but you looked like you were a million miles away."

"Observant, aren't you?" How did one deal with a man like that? Very carefully.

"You'll find out how observant."

Now why didn't that bother her? If any other man had said that to her, she'd be running for the door. Not with Max. He slid the food onto their plates, then took a seat next to her. Sierra took a bite of the eggs and let out a moan. "These are fluffiest eggs I've had outside of a restaurant."

"I'm glad you like them." They ate in silence for a few minutes. "Tell me, Sierra, what kind of childhood did you have?"

She almost choked on the piece of bacon she was eating. "A normal one, I guess." That seemed an odd question to start with unless...oh, hell. "I had a nightmare last night." Her voice was tight and flat. Was she ready to have this conversation with him? Not really. "Did I talk in my sleep?"

Max regarded her over his coffee cup. "Yes, you had a nightmare. Yes, you did talk, but it didn't make sense to me."

He wasn't pulling any punches, and she appreciated his honesty. "Sorry about that." She couldn't remember the nightmare, only how safe she felt, and that had to be because of Max.

"You never did finish telling me how you came to have the club?" She wanted to deflect attention away from her.

"You're changing the subject." Max stared at her. "I recognize what you're doing. Just know that I'll get the answers I want, eventually."

She would deal with it at a later date when her defenses were back at full strength. She nodded, and he continued. "I told you Jordan, Damon, and I were not finding what we wanted. I decided to build a club and run it the way I wanted."

"Why out here?"

"Besides owning the land, it's not that far from downtown Pleasant Valley. This way, I have privacy and security for my home and the club."

"I noticed the gates and call boxes."

"Yes, apparently the gate to the club malfunctioned the night we met. It should have been closed when you walked up. I think the storm messed it up."

"How?" She was curious.

"When I checked the programming, the lights had flickered right before you arrived. There was just enough surge to force the gates open. They're set to open in case of a power failure. A safety feature."

"Nice. So tell me more. Did you have this house built too?"

"Part of it. When I inherited this place from my grandfather, the house was smaller, so I had it remodeled while I had the club built."

"So...private club, very private from what I've seen. Can you tell me more about that?"

"Now I see why you're good at your job."

She tilted her head and looked at him.

"You ask the right questions to keep people talking."

Sierra smiled and ducked her head. "Here's another one. How did the questions you asked me tell you I was submissive?"

His spine straightened and his hazel eyes took on a glow. "The questions are tailored that way. If you had said you preferred being on top, or would rather tie someone up than be tied up, the result would have been different. The night we met, you allowed me to order you around."

"I did, but that doesn't mean I'll allow it all the time." She wrinkled her nose at him. "I have to be strong and not back down to do my job."

He nodded. "There are different types of submissive. You know that, don't you?"

She nodded. "24/7 slave types, bedroom types, club types."

"Correct. Each dynamic is different and determines their choice for themselves. You, sweetheart are a bedroom/club mixture."

"And you got that from the questions?"

"Yes and no." He curved his hand around the back of her neck, and she relaxed into his hold. "Right there. What are you thinking?"

"Nothing really." She was concentrating on him.

"Let's try this: What happened when I put my hand on the back of your neck?"

She blinked. "It was calming."

"Right. Haven't you ever wished you could come home and have someone else take over? Where you don't need to make any decisions?"

"Doesn't every woman?"

"No." He leaned closer and Sierra shifted in her seat. "Already I can see your breathing has increased, and there's a little hitch in your breathing pattern as well. It excites you to think about letting me take over."

Did it? This was interesting.

"Now your brain is getting involved. You're thinking everything through. Let that go. This is more about emotions and feelings than thinking." His fingers played with her hair.

Damn, the man was right. His fingers in her hair caused her nerves to tingle. She wanted to deny it, but couldn't, because he was right. She craved a little time where she didn't have to think about anything.

"Let's try an experiment." He hopped off the stool, helped her off hers, and led her back into the bedroom. "I want you to remove your t-shirt and lie on the bed."

Sierra crossed her arms over her chest. "I'm not sure about this."

"Sierra." He stared at her as his voice dropped. "Go with what you're *feeling*, not what you're thinking. I'm not going to do anything you don't want. You have one minute to take off the shirt and get on that bed before I punish you."

Punish? A shiver of excitement—or was it apprehension—shook her body. Max turned away from her, and she quickly pulled the t-shirt off and laid down on the bed. She arranged her hair so it covered her breasts.

She turned her head to see Max approaching the bed with stuff in his hands. He set the items on the bedside table. A bottle of what looked like massage oil, a feather, and ... she didn't know what the third item was. It looked like a bunch of colored strands bound together.

"Now that won't do, sweetheart." Max sat on the bed, his hip brushing hers. He pushed her hair from her breasts, baring them to his gaze. Sierra squirmed and fought against using her hands to cover them.

"Close your eyes."

There was that voice again. That deep timbre with a hint of steel in it. She took a shuddering breath and closed her eyes.

"Good girl. Now, take a deep breath and let it out."

She wrinkled her nose but did as he said. He had her do it a few times.

"Can you keep your hands at your sides?"

She nodded. Her arms were so relaxed she didn't want to move them anyway.

"I need words."

"Yes, Sir, I can." Where the hell did that sir come from? It was a natural response to his firm tone, and from what she'd read, if she was going to be a sub, she needed to get her head in the right space.

Max chuckled. She jumped when his finger traced the underside of her left breast, then up the outer edge, over the top, through the valley, then he did the same with her right breast.

With each pass, her body sank further and further into the mattress. It was like her bones and muscles had turned to liquid. Slowly the circles became smaller around her nipples, but he didn't touch her nipples.

He kept circling them until, finally, he brushed his thumb over her nipples. Sierra let out a moan. "More," she whispered.

Max gave a husky laugh, then took one nipple and squeezed it. Her legs jerked as her pussy clenched. He did the same to her other nipple. Her stomach clenched and her clit started pulsing.

"Very beautiful breasts," he said softly. "Full, round, and they fit well in my hands." Palms cupped her breasts as if he was weighing them. "Perky nipples, begging for a touch or maybe a kiss."

His lips brushed one and then the other. Sierra squirmed at the pure pleasure flowing through her at his actions. She'd never experienced this deep a connection with any other man. Her back arched when he took her right nipple in his mouth.

"Oh yes, Max...Sir." What were those tiny tingles running all over her body? Her pussy tightened as if it wanted something to hold onto. She was aroused, but it was more than that. Her body was relaxed, and she was enjoying what Max was doing to her.

"I think my pet likes that." His mouth enveloped her other nipple, his tongue flicking it.

Her mouth dropped open as she tried to breathe. Her hips began moving, and she couldn't seem to stop them. Her fingers fisted in the sheet to stop herself from reaching for him.

"Open your eyes."

She did as requested and found him staring at her, heat and desire in his eyes.

"Look down, pet."

Sierra lowered her gaze. Holy crap! Her nipples were bigger than she'd ever seen them. His fingers continued to dance around them, and her nerves danced their own little tango at every touch. She tried to reason this out, but her brain refused to cooperate.

Her skin was flushed with arousal, and she couldn't keep her legs still, even when she tried. Her entire pelvis throbbed with need.

"How can I be—"

"What?" He kissed his way around one breast while his fingers played with the other one, and then he switched sides.

"I..." She couldn't catch her breath. This was crazy.

"Let go, pet," he said in a quiet tone, yet there was a command in his voice.

Sierra shook her head. This was crazy. It couldn't be happening. She'd never climaxed with a man, ever.

"Let go. Now." He pinched both nipples at the same time.

The dam broke, and her climax washed over her. Her legs thrashed against the mattress as she cried out, and her pussy clenched hard. Her gaze locked with his, and she saw satisfaction, and something else.

Sierra closed her eyes as her body stilled. She'd had an orgasm from him just playing with her breasts. And he'd ordered her to come. "I can't believe what just happened." Was that her breathless voice?

"That you climaxed from me playing with your breasts? Or that you came on command?"

"Both." She opened her eyes to see him staring down at her with that damn sexy smile on his face. "Oh, quit looking so satisfied."

His grin widened.

She opened her mouth and her cell rang. "I need my phone."

Max frowned at her. He stood, picked up her purse from where he'd placed it on the chair earlier this morning, opened it and pulled her cell out. He looked at the display and then turned it on. "I'm going to get this for you." Before she could answer he swiped his finger over the screen. She really needed to password protect it. "Hello, this is Max."

"Damn it, Max." Sierra sat up, crossing her arms over her chest. He glared at her, and she glared back. "That's my phone. You have no right. Now give me my phone." She held her hand out.

"Sierra will call you back in a few minutes, Crystal." He tapped the screen.

Sierra glanced at the ceiling, willing herself not to lose it with Max. "You are overstepping your bounds again. You can't keep doing this, Max." His lips were compressed, but she wasn't going to back down. "It isn't right."

"It's not." His voice was quiet. "It looks like I owe you another apology. I seem to act without thinking with you."

"Well, curb that instinct. Especially when we're alone." She waved her hand at him and he placed her cell in her palm. "Thank you."

"I don't know what it is about you. I can't seem to control my protective instincts when it comes to you." He sat down next to her on the bed his shoulders bowed.

"I'd be a liar if I said I don't like your protective instincts, but this overbearing, protective caveman I don't like."

"I'll find a way to tone him down."

"You better, or we're over with." She punched in Crystal's number.

"Hey."

"Oh my God!" Crystal screeched in her ear. "You're with Max."

"Yes, we had dinner together last night." Sierra rolled her eyes. Why the hell did she tell Crystal that? "Look, I really can't talk right now."

"Oh, did I interrupt you two in a delicate situation?"

"To be honest, yes. Bye, Crystal." Sierra hit the *end* button and tossed her phone on the side table. "I have to move now and find a new best friend." Crystal was going to insist on hearing the full story.

Max chuckled. *Well, at least someone's mood improved.*

"Where did that t-shirt go?" She turned to look for it, but froze when Max put his hand on her shoulder.

"When did my straight-laced Sierra get this?" His fingers caressed the skin on her back, right at her shoulder blade.

"College dare." She liked she could surprise him. "It's just a tattoo."

"It's a butterfly with fairy wings done in beautiful colors. It suits you."

"Thank you. Now, I'd like to cover up."

"I like you half-naked."

Sierra blew out a breath.

"Just for a few more minutes, please. Come on." He tugged her to her feet and led her over to the sitting area in his bedroom. He sat down in an overstuffed chair and pulled her into his lap.

"I can sit on my own." She tried to wriggle out of his lap, and he tightened his arms around her.

"I know you can. Why were you so surprised you climaxed?"

"We are not going there, Max." She glared at him. "Release me now." When he did as she asked, she almost fell off his lap. Sierra stood, found the t-shirt and slipped it on. "What we're going to talk about instead is you violating my consent and disregard for personal boundaries." She took a breath. "You may be a Dom in your club and your home, but you haven't earned the privilege of being *my dominant*, not yet. I've read the book you gave me as well as others on the list. Some of your actions are direct violations of consent. What do you have to say for yourself?"

His eyes darkened. "You're right. I'm being a bad Dom. And I know better." He leaned forward and laid his hands on his knees. He took a deep breath. "I do want to be your Dom."

"Then follow the rules. Can we agree on that?" Her body vibrated. She didn't like confrontation, but she had to do this; otherwise, Max could walk all over her. This was her life.

"We can." He held his hands out in front of him. "As a Dom it is my responsibility to make sure you and I both know the rules. I've fallen down on the job."

"What do you suggest?" she asked. At least he was listening to her.

"Let's both get dressed and go into the family room. We sit down and go over rules for our Dom/sub relationship along with the club rules. Then we can set boundaries in our personal relationship too."

His idea had merit. They really never talked about rules for their relationship. As for the club, she remembered reading them, but not much beyond that. "Agreed."

"Okay. Your clothes are in the bathroom. I ran them through the laundry."

"When?"

"Earlier this morning. You were sleeping soundly and didn't even notice when I got up."

"You're sneaky, Max."

"You have no idea." He slapped her on the ass as she walked by, and instead of feeling offended, Sierra exaggerated her walk and the sound of his laughter made her smile.

Fifteen minutes later, when she walked into the family room, Max was settled on the sofa, dressed in black pants and a navy blue t-shirt. He was breathtaking. There were two note pads, pens and a file folder sitting on the coffee table.

"Come sit down." He patted the cushion next to him.

Sierra bit her lip to stop from smiling. This man always trying to get her close. Well, right now, she needed some distance. She marched over and sat in the overstuffed chair.

"I see." His eyebrows rose. Max shifted the items on the coffee table closer to her before he shifted closer to her. "I respect your decision."

"Thank you." Maybe her words from earlier sunk in. "What is all this?" She waved her hand at the paper and pens on the table.

"So we can both take notes, and I brought your folder from the club so we could also go over the club rules."

"Can we start with those?" She'd feel more comfortable talking about those rules before they got to personal rules.

"Sure." Max flipped open the folder. "What do you remember of the rules?"

Sierra swallowed. "No drugs, alcohol, or cell phones in the club." Those were the easy ones. "No means no." She closed her eyes trying to picture the rules. She'd read them more than once, so it shouldn't be that hard. "Report problems. Food and beverages only in allowed areas, no smoking, clean up after yourselves." She paused.

"Very good. Do you remember the others?"

"I don't." She opened her eyes to see Max watching her. She started to shift in her seat at his molten gaze, but stopped herself.

"You got the ones I expected you to remember. What about safe words?"

"Yellow and red." Those she remembered.

"What kind of play is not allowed in the club?"

This time she did shift in her seat. "I don't remember."

Max's lips turned up. "No breath play, cutting, humiliation, needles, scat play or golden showers."

"How could I forget that?" Especially the breath play. She shivered.

"It takes time." He leaned back. "Edge play and fire play are allowed on a case by case basis, usually only for demonstration purposes."

Sierra's foot began tapping against the carpet. Those were two things that scared the crap out of her. She almost laughed, the only two? There was a lot more than that, but those were the main two.

"How do you address others in the club?"

She wrinkled her nose. "Sir or Ma'am for a Dom or Domme. With subs, I can use their name if I know it."

He nodded. "Do you remember what you need to wear?"

She drew her lower lip between her teeth. She'd planned on reviewing the rules before they went into the club the first time. "I don't."

"This isn't a test." Max's words were soft. "It takes time. Club rules state a female sub can wear a light top, bra or nothing."

Her breath caught in her throat. Nothing? "You don't expect..." She couldn't even get the words out.

113

"I'll work with what you're comfortable with. Can we go with light top or bra?"

She nodded.

Max reached and picked up a pad of paper and a pen and scribbled on the paper. "Skirt, shorts or nothing. What's your choice?"

"Skirt, maybe shorts." Sierra looked down. What was she thinking? She couldn't show her body off. The scratching of a pen across paper was the only noise in the room.

"Do you have any issues going barefoot?"

"Is that even sanitary?"

"The floors are disinfected and sanitized every night. I had specialized flooring installed that is easy to keep clean. Plus it's padded."

"So no shoes."

"If you want to wear high heels, that would be okay. Or do you have a medical condition with your feet?"

"No heels." She never wore high heels. Heck none of her shoes were over an inch high, and even then they were wedges. "I can do bare feet."

His pen moved again. "That does it for the club rules. Are you ready for personal?"

"I guess." Her foot tapped faster.

"Sierra." At Max's tone, she lifted her head. His expression held concern. "If you don't want to do this, tell me, and that will be the end of it."

She shook her head. "I want to do this." Her voice was barely above a whisper. She took a deep breath. "This is very different. I've never really had a discussion like this with any man."

"I'm not surprised." Max sat forward, resting his elbows on his knees. "Communication in any relationship is important, but more so in kink. I skipped this step, and I shouldn't have. We've talked but not about the important stuff."

She nodded. "Right. Okay." Another deep breath. "No dominant stuff outside the bedroom or club. I make my own decisions."

His lips turned up. "Agreed. And if I step out of line, you tell me."

"Like I did today."

"Yes, if it comes to that." He rubbed his chin. "I'll admit that sometimes my dominant side comes out and I lose all perspective."

"I see. You'll just have to learn I'm not a pushover."

"Noted." He scribbled on the paper. "Bedroom and club. Are you okay with all the normal dating stuff? Dinner, picnics, just hanging out together?"

"Yes." Breathing was becoming easier.

"Let's talk about bedroom play."

Her breath hitched, and Sierra shifted in her seat. "All right." Damn, was that her breathy voice.

"How do you feel about erotic talk?"

She tilted her head. "What do you mean?"

"If I use words like fuck, pussy, tits, ass. Do those bother you?"

"No."

"Cunt."

"Oh, hell no." She started to stand.

"No humiliation-type of words." He scribbled another note.

Sierra collapsed back onto the chair with a pounding heart. "No. I don't react well to that word or others like it." Too close to the way her father treated her.

"Noted." He scribbled on the paper. "Phone sex?"

Her stomach fluttered. "That should be okay."

"Oral sex?"

Heat began moving up her body from her toes. "Yes, please."

Max glanced up from the paper. "Giving and receiving?"

She shifted in her seat. "Yes."

"I want to go over your questionnaire for the club. Are you okay with toys in the bedroom?"

Her foot began tapping again. "Depending on the toy, yes. I would like to know what you would use on me." More flutters in her stomach.

"I can do that. Right now I'm thinking mainly of vibrators, dildos, bullets, blindfold, and nipple clamps."

Heat crept up her neck. "I can agree to those."

"What about positions?"

"Positions?" She tilted her head and stared at him.

"Sexual positions."

The heat hit her cheeks. "Oh. I never thought about it." Wasn't that the truth. "I'm not very worldly, am I?" she asked in a soft voice as she looked down at her tapping foot.

"Sierra." Max's voice was soft but firm. "Please look at me."

Taking a breath, she lifted her head and looked at him. He was watching her with those hazel eyes of his. Actually he was studying her.

"Communication goes both ways. Asking me a question because I've said something you're not quite sure of is nothing to be embarrassed or upset about. We all have different experiences in our lives. Good and bad."

"Gotcha." She forced her foot still. "I've only ever done missionary."

"All right. Are you open to doggie style? Standing? Other positions?"

"As long as you're not looking to do something crazy like downward dog, I think I'm okay."

His laugh was rich and full. "I'll note, no aerobatic positions." His pen moved over the paper once again. "From your questionnaire, would most of that hold true in the bedroom?"

"I need to see my questionnaire."

He leaned over and picked up the folder and handed it to her. Sierra located the papers and flipped through the pages. "Yes, I believe these are all fine in the bedroom."

"Okay. How do you feel about sex in different places?"

"Like in public?" She was already shaking her head.

"I mean here in the house. In different rooms, out by the pool, in the pool?"

"Oh." A giggle bubbled up. "Sorry." Where the heck had that come from? "Those are fine."

"How would you feel about sex in the club?" He held up his hand when she opened her mouth. "When you're ready. I'm not talking right away. We're building a relationship here. Not everything will be done right away."

Her cheeks were hot. "We will talk about it before we do it?"

117

His hand covered hers where it rested on the arm of the chair. "We will always talk. I might have messed up, but now I'm back on the straight and narrow."

"Okay." She blew out a breath.

"Good. Now I have a question that is probably going to make you uncomfortable, but I think it's important."

Sierra pressed her lips together and waited.

"Will you tell me why you were so surprised you climaxed earlier?"

This time the heat went clear to her scalp, and she glanced over his shoulder. How did she explain this one? He'd asked her, but it didn't mean she had to answer. However, it was important. "I don't orgasm easily." She barely whispered the words as she pulled her hand from his and wrapped her arms around her waist.

Silence descended. Damn, she shouldn't have said anything. Just told him it was none of his business. Communication. It was important. All the books talked about it.

"I'm sorry. Did you say you don't climax easily?"

On hearing the disbelief in his voice, she lifted her head. There was no censure in his eyes or his face.

"That's right." Her voice was louder and steadier this time.

"You've never climaxed during sex?"

Her body trembled. "No, I haven't."

"By your own hand?"

"Sometimes." Her face was so hot now, she'd bet she was getting a sunburn.

"Toys."

"A vibrator. Once."

"I see."

Those two words went straight to her heart. "I'm sorry," she whispered once again. "I'm defective."

"Like hell you are." His fierce words hit her upside the head. The pad of paper and pen clattered on the table, and then Max was kneeling next to her chair, his palms framing her face. "Sweetheart, you are not defective. Some women have trouble climaxing. And while I don't believe you're one of them, I believe the men in your life never took time to understand you or your body."

His words soothed the fear in her heart.

"You checked off you're okay with light bondage."

"Yes." She shifted her feet.

"At the club and when we're alone?"

Her stomach fluttered. "Yes." Oh Lord, her nerves tingled at the thought of being tied up and at Max's mercy.

"We're going to be just fine together. I have one last question for you?"

"Okay." She didn't know how much more she could take. Her body was at odds with itself. Hot, trembling, scared, excited.

"How did it feel when I took command of you and your body?"

"Like freedom." The word slipped from her lips. She'd felt free. In a place where she didn't have to make decisions or worry about anything, that was, until her cell rang.

"Perfect." He rubbed his fingers over her cheeks. "Freedom is a good feeling."

"Yeah." She blinked then glanced over at the TV, which displayed the time. "Oh my goodness, is it that late?"

Max followed her gaze. "Yep. I suspect I need to get you home before Crystal sends out a search party."

"That would be nice."

"Then let's go, my lady." He stood and brought her to her feet. "It will be okay, Sierra. We have a foundation now. A starting point." He dropped a kiss on her nose. "We're going to have a lot of fun, you and I."

Her mouth went dry and her breathing increased. She was going to have a kink relationship with Max. Her body quivered in a good way.

Chapter Nine

Sierra closed the door to her apartment and leaned against it. Her brain was muddled, confused, and satisfied. A knock on the door behind her made her jump. Crystal.

"Spill, woman," Crystal said pushing her way into the apartment, carrying a bag in her hand. "Ice cream and cookies. Wasn't sure which was appropriate."

"Both probably. Let me go change clothes."

Crystal frowned at her. "Those are the clothes you were wearing yesterday."

"Yep. Give me five." Sierra went into her bedroom and found a pair of sweats and a t-shirt. A yawn escaped. Lord she was tired. "Hey Crystal, I'm going to lie down for a few minutes."

"Okay. But I'm bouncing waiting to talk."

Sierra laughed and lay down. A twenty-minute power nap and she'd be ready to talk with Crystal.

* * * *

Max finished up the last of the paperwork he needed to do and rubbed his eyes. The club was cleaned, and he totaled up the damage. Cook wouldn't be happy, but that wasn't Max's problem. It was almost four. He'd taken Sierra home at one and already missed her. He reached for his phone and dialed.

"Sierra's phone," a quiet female voice said.

"Hi. This is Max. Can I talk to Sierra, please?"

"Oh hi. This is Crystal." There was noise on the other end as if Crystal was walking. "Trying to be quiet. Sierra is taking a nap right now. I can take a message."

A nap. That didn't surprise him. She hadn't slept well last night, and between her orgasm and their talk, he'd worn her out. "Just let her know I called."

"Will do. We're going to have a girls' night tonight, complete with Graziano's pizza. Our favorite place."

Now why was she telling him this? "Good. She needs a night at home. Thank you, Crystal. Enjoy girls' night."

Max hung up the phone and an idea popped into his head. He pulled up the internet on his computer and found the number he wanted.

* * * *

Sierra staggered out of bed, disoriented.

"It's about time you woke up." Crystal said from the doorway.

"What time is it?" She sat up and pushed her hair away from her face. That's twice now she'd lain down without braiding it.

"Almost five."

"I slept for almost four hours?"

"Yep. Tessa is on her way over. I put the ice cream in the freezer. I decided we needed a girls' night. So in a bit, I'll order Graziano's, but first, you need to get your lazy ass up."

Sierra stood and stretched. "I'm sorry I fell asleep like that. I only intended to rest for a few minutes."

"No worries. I chilled and watched TV." The doorbell rang. "That should be Tessa. Freshen up and then come out, and you call tell both of us about your adventure."

When Sierra walked into her living room, Tessa and Crystal were sitting on the sofa chatting. An open bottle of red wine sat on the table with three glasses.

Sierra plopped down on her worn forest green chair and smiled. "Hey, Tessa."

"I brought wine. Crystal said we might need it."

"She did?" Sierra looked at her other friend.

"Yes, now spill about last night." Crystal grabbed a glass of wine.

"When I came out of work yesterday, Max was leaning against my vehicle."

"Just waiting for you?"

"Yep. He invited me to dinner." Sierra picked up her own glass of wine and sat back in the soft chair, curling her legs beneath her.

"And you accepted?" The disbelief in Tessa's voice made Sierra smile.

"I did. Mainly because I was curious why he showed up, but also because..." How much should she disclose to her friends?

"Because?" Crystal sat forward.

Sierra hesitated. She'd signed an NDA. "Let me think for a minute. I signed an NDA."

"What?" Crystal sat up. "Tell me about this NDA. You should have had me read it."

"Easy, Crystal." Tessa patted her arm. "I'm sure Sierra knows what she's doing."

"Like hell. NDAs are not always enforceable. I want to know what it said."

Crystal was a paralegal and was a great source of information. "I signed it two weeks ago, and I do have a copy somewhere. It was no big deal." Sierra closed her eyes and thought back. "All right. I have it now. I was curious about how Max decided to open a BDSM club."

Tessa's mouth dropped opened and Crystal's eyes gleamed. "Oh my god! Is it anything like the books we read?" Crystal asked.

"I haven't been inside the actual club yet." There was nothing in the NDA that said she couldn't talk about the club, just she couldn't talk about the members or what a particular member did inside the club. Besides, these were her friends.

"Explain," Crystal demanded.

Tessa looked a little shell-shocked, but there was a gleam of curiosity in her brown gaze.

"I only saw the entrance, bathroom, and Max's office that night you picked me up. The other two times I've been there we've been in the classroom."

"You went back for classes. Spill it all. Now." Crystal set her wine glass down and rubbed her hands together.

"I went back because Max invited me. It was a class, an introduction to the club in a way."

"Were there other people there?" Tessa asked.

"Yes, we started with eight of us by the end there was only three of us."

"Why so few?" Crystal frowned.

"A lot of it had to do with the requirements. Not only was there the NDA, but you had to approve a background check, read the rules, and fill out a questionnaire about your past experience."

"Like what?" Tessa asked as the doorbell rang again.

"Who could that be?" Sierra stood, and went to the door. She looked out the peephole and then opened the door.

"Hey Sierra. Here's your order," Johnny, the pizza delivery guy, said. His blond hair was mussed.

"Hey Johnny." Sierra turned. "Crystal, come help. Food is here."

"What?" Crystal came over to the door.

Johnny handed the food to Crystal and turned to walk away. "Hey wait, I need to pay you." Sierra said.

"All taken care of. Have a good evening." The kid jogged away.

Sierra closed the door and looked at Crystal. "I thought you hadn't ordered yet."

"Who cares?" Tessa said. "I'm starving and that garlic bread smells heavenly."

It did. Together, the three trooped into her kitchen. Sierra grabbed the plates, while Tessa grabbed napkins, and Crystal opened the food.

All their favorites. Cheesy garlic bread, Caesar salad, and meat-lovers pizza with extra cheese. Sierra's stomach growled, and they all laughed.

"Breakfast was a long time ago." It had been.

"Ah, there's a note here for you, Sierra." Crystal pulled a white piece of paper off the side of the salad container.

A note from the pizza place? Sierra took it and opened it.

Sierra, I hope you and your friends have a wonderful girls' night. Your friend Crystal mentioned pizza from Graziano's was your favorite, so I called and had them send over your normal order. Enjoy. P.S., I'll pick you up Saturday night at seven, and a package will be delivered on Saturday with what you should wear. Max.

Sierra's breathing hitched. He'd ordered them food, and he wanted her to wear an outfit he picked out next Saturday. Wait. That's the new member club night. Oh, Lord, her heart pounded and her nipples grew hard.

"When did you talk to Max?" Sierra stared at Crystal, trying to take her mind off what Max was sending her to wear.

Crystal's hand paused as she was reaching for a piece of pizza. "He called while you were sleeping." Her face turned pink. "I picked up your phone so it wouldn't wake you up. Sorry."

"Wait a second; are you saying Max sent the pizza?" Tessa asked.

"Yes." Sierra waved the note. "Apparently, Crystal told him we were having girls' night and getting pizza from Graziano's. He called and asked that our normal order be delivered."

"Sorry." Crystal's voice was soft. "I really didn't think about what I was saying outside of I wanted him to know you were busy tonight."

"So Max paid for our pizza and had it delivered. I'm not sure if its romantic or not," Tessa said.

"It sounds just like Max." Sierra folded the note and set it on the table. "He's...well, I wouldn't call him a nurturer. He's...We're learning together. He's been a little too aggressive, but we talked. He promised to tone it down." She'd have to discuss this with him. "In some of the books we read the men like to take care of their women. Max is like that, sometimes he crosses the line."

"Well, I did tell him about it. So he took the initiative to make sure we all had food tonight."

"Oh hell," Tessa said her eyes softening. "That's so damn romantic."

"Maybe." Sierra tapped her fingers against her lips. She was touched that Max saw to it they had food, but also a bit annoyed he did it without asking, but then it wouldn't have been a surprise.

She let out a sigh. So many things they needed to navigate in this relationship, things she never even thought about.

They filled their plates and then went into the living room. "So the questionnaire you filled out..." Crystal said, waving a piece of garlic bread at Sierra.

"It was very detailed." Sierra took a bite of salad first. She really didn't need the carbs from the bread and pizza, but heck, you only live once.

"What did it ask?" Tessa took a bite of her pizza and let out a moan. "Damn, I love this stuff."

"Ummm." Sierra wondered how to say this. It wasn't like the three hadn't talked about sex or stuff. Hell, the books Tessa brought for her to read were sometimes close to erotica, but never crossed that line. Erotic romance at its best.

"Your cheeks are turning pink. What has embarrassed you so much?" Crystal asked.

127

"The books we've read never really go into details. They just mention check lists and stuff like that." Sierra took a sip of wine. "It asked about everything sexual you could ever think of. If you wanted to do it, might want to do it, or never want to do it."

Tessa let out a choking sound. "Oh my god. You filled out your hard limits."

"Yep." Sierra didn't read as fast as Tessa and Crystal. She'd read the books they loaned, but she never thought she'd find someone like that. Maybe because the men she dated seemed to be asses.

"This is getting better and better," Crystal said.

"Yeah. I've gone through two classes. Yesterday, when I got out of work, Max was waiting for me. He asked me to dinner. I accepted so I could talk to him more about the club, and then we got interrupted." How much did she want to divulge? These were her friends, she could tell them anything. "Max got a phone call."

"What happened?" Crystal asked.

"Well, there was a private party at the club, and let's just say they weren't following the rules."

"That sounds interesting," Tessa polished off her food and set her plate on the coffee table before picking up her wine.

"Yeah. I was waiting for Max in the registration area when this big guy came lumbering in. I could tell he was high and drunk, something not allowed there."

"Oh crap," Tessa said.

"Shit." Crystal put her food down and touched Sierra's arm. "Are you okay?"

"Yes." They knew about her father and his drunken rages. "The man grabbed me, and I kicked him in the balls and then screamed. Max was there in a second with help." A shiver went through her body. What if Max hadn't heard her scream? Who was she kidding? She could bring a house down with her scream, something self-defense had taught her.

Then why hadn't she screamed with Carl? Maybe because she didn't think he'd turn violent. She'd puzzle that out later. "Max had the guy removed and took me to his office while he took care of the issues in the club. Then, when he was done, he took me to his place instead of home."

"Good man," Crystal said.

"What?" Sierra's mouth fell open.

"I agree with Crystal," Tessa said.

"You didn't need to be alone, and I know you wouldn't have called me. That man grabbing you was a traumatic episode and probably gave you a flashback to your childhood," Crystal explained.

"Yeah." Sierra let out a sigh. "Anyway, I broke down and Max held me while I cried. Then he gave me a change of clothes and put me to bed. This morning, he made me breakfast, we talked, and he brought me home." Sierra stared down at her plate. She didn't mention how Max had brought her to climax by just playing with her breasts. Her brain was still trying to process it all, and her breasts still tingled from his fingers.

"I think I like this man," Tessa commented.

"Maybe, but I want to check him out. When are you seeing him again?" Crystal asked.

"Next Saturday." Sierra clamped her hand over her mouth. Damn it.

Crystal's eyes gleamed. "Oh good, I can check him out."

Chapter Ten

The next week passed quickly. Thursday night class was basically a walkthrough of what they could expect in the club on Saturday. They'd been given a tour of the club and the equipment. Her stomach was still buzzing with nerves. Now it was Saturday, and she eyed the white box that had been delivered like it was a snake ready to strike. She'd kept herself busy today by cleaning and doing laundry.

Crystal had called twice, telling Sierra she wanted to be there for safety reasons when Max picked her up. Sierra laughed. If she hadn't felt safe with Max, she wouldn't have gone out with him or to his home.

She did feel safe with Max. There was something about him that she trusted. It could be his confidence, or arrogance, as some might call it.

Quit being a chicken and open the damn box.

Sierra pulled the end of the ribbon, releasing the bow, and set the ribbon aside. She lifted the lid to reveal lavender tissue paper and an envelope with her name on it.

Opening the envelope, she pulled out the piece of paper.

Sierra,

This is the outfit you will wear tonight at the club. Just the outfit, no underwear. You may choose a jacket or coat to cover you, but once we get to the club, the outerwear will be removed. Footwear is up to you, but at the club, you will be barefoot. I look forward to seeing you.
Max

Wait, no underwear? She vaguely remembered there was something in the rules about shoes, but clothing? Damn, she really needed to read her copy of the paperwork. She parted the tissue paper and froze.

On top lay a light purple sheer lace garment that would hide nothing. She lifted it out of the box by the two dainty straps tied into bows. Undo those, and the entire bodice would fall.

She remembered how much Max enjoyed playing with her breasts the other night. Heat filled her. Next, was a long black skirt. Sierra pulled it out. This didn't look so bad. Was she ready for this?

She glanced at the clock. It was five already. Oh lord, she needed help. She snatched up her phone. "Get over here," she said to Crystal then hung up. Five minutes later, Crystal rang her doorbell.

"So good sense finally hit you over the head," Crystal said, breezing into her apartment.

"Yes, and no." She shut the door and then pulled Crystal into her bedroom. "Help." She gestured to the outfit on her bed.

Crystal whistled. "Club clothing." Crystal turned and put her hands on her hips. "Hair up, into the shower, and shave. Go."

Sierra didn't even hesitate. She followed Crystal orders. Why was she even thinking about wearing these clothes? Maybe because she wanted to see if the freedom she'd felt in Max's arms last week could be repeated.

It was more than that. She wanted Max. She wanted to be with him and in his bed. She'd always regret it if she didn't find out where this could lead. She might scoff at the romance books she'd read, but damn it…she did want to see if the things she'd read about were real.

By the time she came out in her robe, Crystal had arranged her makeup table. "Come sit." She patted the chair. Sierra padded over and sat down. "Subtle makeup, and I think we'll braid your hair; that will keep it out of the way."

Sierra remained still while Crystal worked. When she was done, Sierra studied herself in the mirror. "Nice."

"Thanks. Now let's get you into these clothes."

Sierra stood, undid her robe, and threw it on the bed. Crystal raised her eyebrows. "Underwear."

"I'm not allowed."

Crystal stopped and stared.

"It's okay, Crystal," Sierra reassured her friend. "I want to do this."

"Okay." Crystal held the top out. "If you're sure."

"I am." Sierra took the top and slipped it on.

The lace was soft and caressed her skin. Crystal handed her the skirt. She slipped it on. Wait a second; something was different. Sierra turned and noticed the slit down each side.

She took a step. "Oh lordy," she whispered.

"What?" Crystal looked down. "Holy crap."

"I can't wear this." The top was bad enough, but the slits on the sides of the skirt went from hem to waist.

"Sierra." Crystal's tone was low. "You can do this." Crystal grasped her by the shoulders. "This is just like the books we read."

"But men don't act like that in real life."

"Apparently, they do." Crystal squeezed her shoulder. "You look sexy as hell."

Sierra turned and looked at herself in the full-length mirror on the bathroom door. "Is that really me?" Color was high in her cheeks, but it didn't detract from the way her eyes glowed.

The top clung to her body, only hinting at the nakedness beneath it. As for the skirt, it hugged her waist, and if she didn't walk no one would even know the slits were there.

She took a couple of steps, watching herself in the mirror. It showed off her legs, her entire leg, but that was it. Sierra took a shuddering breath.

"You are gorgeous. Not that you weren't always a looker, but this outfit...I don't know what to say." Crystal came up behind her. "If you don't do this, you'll always wonder."

"I know." Max picked out the outfit and he knew what he was doing. "I need shoes."

She did. "In the back, there's a pair of black stilettos." She'd bought them years ago, and while she told Max she didn't like heels, tonight called for them. At least this first night of them being together.

"Okay." Crystal went over to her closet. "There they are." Crystal backed out and held them up. "These are perfect."

They were.

The shoes were made of leather that molded to her feet. The heel was a little over an inch high, which was the reason she'd bought them in the first place. Comfortable, yet there was a support in the bottom. Crystal slipped them on Sierra's feet and then stepped back.

"But you can't go out like this. You'll be arrested."

"True. I have a raincoat." She'd bought it in the spring when they were on sale, knowing she'd need it this winter.

"Found it." Crystal draped it over her arm. "It's five to seven, shall we go wait for Max?"

The doorbell rang just as they walked into the living room. Sierra took a deep breath as she carefully walked to the door. It had been a long time since she wore heels. After checking who it was, she opened the door. Max stood there in a pair of black pants and black shirt.

His gaze went from her head to her toes. "Fuck. You are perfect," he said, his eyes gleaming with appreciation.

"Thank you." Her nerves danced. "Come in for a minute. Crystal wants to formally meet you."

He stepped inside, and Sierra closed the door, her heart pounding. Why was she so nervous?

"I'm Crystal, we've talked on the phone. And you'd better not hurt Sierra."

"Crystal." Sierra shook her head. She couldn't believe what her best friend had said.

Max smiled. He pulled a card out of his pocket. "This is my friend Jordan. Call him if you're worried." His voice was firm and no-nonsense. "I won't hurt Sierra." He paused and looked at her. The passion in his eyes stole Sierra's breath. "Unless she asks me to."

Heat flared over Sierra's body. Her knees wobbled.

"Good enough for me." Crystal walked over to her. "Call me when you get home, no matter what time it is." Crystal leaned closer. "He's delicious. Text me with our code word when you get to the club and when you leave." Crystal straightened. "Have fun." She opened the door and then closed it behind her.

"And that was Crystal."

Max laughed. "She's a good friend. Do you have a jacket?"

"Yes." Sierra picked up her raincoat from the back of the sofa.

Max took it and held it out so she could slip her arms into it. "I'm glad you have this," he whispered.

"You are?"

"Yes. It puts the temptation of your creamy flesh out of sight until we get to the club." His gaze swept over her. "I can't believe you wore heels."

More heat flared. Sierra grabbed her purse, not that the small one had much in it. Only her wallet and cell phone. "Just until we get to the club. I remember you said barefoot in your note." She grabbed her keys off the hook, and Max opened the door. After she locked her apartment, he guided her to his SUV and helped her into it.

Sierra twisted her hands in her lap as Max drove. When they left the city, he reached over, pried her hands apart, and held one in his. "Why are you so nervous?"

"You've seen how I'm dressed." She swallowed. Maybe she wasn't ready for this step.

"Sweetheart, you're beautiful." He squeezed her hand.

"I don't know if I can do this." Her stomach was a tangled mess.

"You can." His voice was calm and steady, which helped her. "Remember, I will be by your side. Tonight is for you to get a feel for the club. We're not doing a scene tonight. I want you to see what goes on."

Sierra let out a big sigh. "I'd forgotten." With everything going on, she'd forgotten tonight was for the new members to get their feet wet, so to speak. Jordan would be monitoring the couple who'd been in the class with her.

"Then let's review a bit. Club safe words?"

"Red to stop, yellow to slow down."

"Good. If a Dom or Domme asks you to play?"

"I have the right to say no, and they are required to accept it."

"Right. Even though I'll be at your side, I might get called away, so always remember you can just say no. If someone doesn't listen, yell red."

A shiver swept over Sierra as she remembered the man who grabbed her at the club. "Will a member disregard my no?"

"They shouldn't, but even with our screening process people still slip through. I just want you prepared." He glanced over at her. "What happened with that private party was an anomaly."

"Okay."

"Last thing. What do you call the Doms?"

"Sir or Master as directed, but always start with Sir."

"And the Dommes?"

"Ma'am unless directed otherwise." At least she remembered all that.

"Tonight is a chance for you to observe and firm up your soft limits and hard limits. You might not see everything here tonight, but it will give you a good feel."

137

Sierra nodded as he turned his car up the driveway to his house. "I thought we were going to the club."

"We are." Max parked the vehicle and then helped her down. "There's a pathway from my house to the club." He took her hand and led her to the back of the house and opened the electronic gate.

The pathway led past the back of the house, past the patio and pool. Then they came to the back of the club. Another electronic lock, and Max was pulling the door open.

Sierra recognized that they were near the classroom and Max's office. He led her down the hallway, past the club entrance and bathrooms, to the foyer.

Ralph was there. "Evening, boss, Miss Sierra." Ralph was dressed in a white t-shirt and black jeans.

"Ralph. Go ahead and sign Sierra in. Who is here?"

"Regina and Samantha have checked in. Damon is here and so is Jordan. The Websters are here. I expect others will be arriving shortly." Ralph pulled out a black wristband and a white one and handed them to Max.

"Good." Max took the black band and slipped it on, then slipped the white one on her wrist. "Any issues, let me know," he said to Ralph, then guided her to the entrance of the women's bathroom. "Go in and put your coat and purse in a locker. They're set to your thumbprint, if you have a problem, just ask Regina or Samantha to help you. Once you're ready, come into the club." He cupped her cheek. "Don't overthink this. And if you're not in there in ten minutes, I will come and get you." He turned her to the door and gave her a little push.

Sierra watched over her shoulder as Max sauntered into the club. Damn, the man's ass was sexy as hell. She walked into the bathroom. She'd forgotten how big this facility was. Not only did it have full showers and changing areas, but also a row of lockers and shelves filled with towels.

"Hi, Sierra," Regina said.

"Hi." Sierra smiled at her.

"Max told us to expect you." Regina grinned. "This is Samantha, she's one of the club subs, like me."

"Hello."

Samantha looked at her with cold blue eyes, snorted, and stomped out of the room. What was that all about? Then Sierra realized Samantha was only wearing a thong. Nothing else.

Sierra turned to Regina, who was dressed in a short skirt and a black and red corset. "Just ignore her; she's had a bad day. Do you need some help?"

"Max told me to find a locker and put my stuff in it." Sierra's stomach clenched. Samantha looked like a model, skinny and toned, and Regina was skinnier than her. Damn, was she crazy? She didn't have the type of body to show off to others.

"Okay, here. Use the one next to mine. Just put your purse and coat in there. We're not allowed to carry anything into the club. Oh and you need to remove your shoes."

Sierra frowned. "Remove my shoes?"

"Yes, one of the rules. Only heels or bare feet. I prefer bare feet. Heels kill me after a while."

That's right. Max told her she'd be barefoot. She toed off her shoes and put them in the locker with her purse, but she hesitated when it was time to undo her coat.

Was she really going to go into the club where anyone could see her? "I don't know if I can do this."

"Hey." Regina touched her on the hand. "It's okay; just breathe."

What was she going to do? She didn't want to disappoint Max, but...God, she didn't look anything like Regina or Samantha. Her father's voice, telling her how fat she was, played on a loop in her brain.

"Sierra?" She barely heard Regina's voice.

She couldn't catch her breath. This wasn't going to go well. Max would see right through her. Sierra needed to get out of here. Her body trembled as she turned. Why couldn't she breathe? Ice invaded her veins and her vision wavered.

****

Max stormed into the ladies' room. "What the fuck?"

"I think she's having a panic attack," Regina told him, her eyes full of worry.

"I didn't mean to yell." Max took Sierra by the shoulders. Tremors shook her body, and her eyes were unfocused. Oh yes, his little subbie was having one hell of a panic attack. "Sierra." No response. "Sweetheart." He guided her over to the bench and helped her sit, then he knelt in front of her and took her hands in his.

Sierra blinked.

"Breathe in, and then out," he said softly, doing exactly what he told her to do. "Focus on me. Breathe in, breathe out." He repeated. She inhaled a shuddering breath and then let it out. "That's it. Now again."

140

Regina stood by, her hands clasped together. Max kept his focus on Sierra. "That's it. In and out. Good. Now close your eyes." Sierra did as he asked, and Max's muscles relaxed. She was responding to him. "Picture yourself sitting on grass, by a waterfall, with only the sound of the water and birds."

"Peaceful," she whispered.

Max's gaze remained on Sierra. Her breathing was easier now, her body not as tense. He looked over at Regina. "She'll be fine. Would you please go get me some orange juice from the bar and tell Master Jordan I'm going to be gone for a bit."

"Yes, Master Max." Regina scurried out of the room.

Max rubbed Sierra's hands. "Can you tell me what triggered your panic attack?"

Her eyes didn't open, and there was a slight stiffening of her body, then she sighed. "I'm fat."

Max barely prevented himself from yelling his denial of her statement. His little subbie was full of triggers, and there was no way he could anticipate all of them. They would have to work on them one at a time.

"Sierra, open your eyes." He waited until he saw her baby blue eyes. "You are not fat. You have a beautiful figure, one that I adore."

Her cheeks turned pink. "I don't know if I can do this, Max. I want to, but damn it, I hate being scared. This isn't like me."

"Hey." He cupped her cheek. "One step at a time. You put the outfit on. What did you think at that time?"

"That it showed way too much."

He grinned. "Okay. What else?"

"Crystal was there. She told me I looked good and wanted me to have fun tonight."

"I like your friend."

Regina rushed back into the room. "Master Jordan wanted me to tell you others are arriving and will need the facilities shortly." She held out the glass of juice.

Max nodded. "Tell him five minutes, and thank you." He took the glass from her and held it up to Sierra. "I want you to drink this."

Her hand shook when she took the glass, but she drank the contents. Max took the empty glass from her and pulled her to her feet. "I don't know about the men in your past, but they were asses if they said you were fat." He undid the belt holding her coat shut. "You are anything but." The front of the coat fell open, and his mouth watered.

He guided Sierra over to one of the full-length mirrors on the wall next to the lockers. "Look at the mirror, Sierra." He dropped his voice and made it an order.

She obeyed, and their gazes met in the glass.

"This is what I see. The woman I want to know better." As he talked, he peeled the jacket off of her. "The lace caressing her full breasts, her nipples will soon be rubbing against the fabric in arousal." He tossed the coat over the bench, then put his palms on her hips. "And this skirt, it shows off your long legs. Legs I can't wait to have wrapped around me when we fuck."

"Max." There was shock in her voice, but she didn't pull away from him. Progress.

"Remember club rules."

"Yes, Sir Max."

"Now, let's put your coat in the locker and go out into the club where I can show you off. The women will be jealous and the men will lust after you." He brushed a kiss over her cheek before releasing her.

Max picked up her coat and looked at Sierra. She was still standing in front of the mirror, turning from left to right. He smiled. Crisis averted. He put her coat in the locker then beckoned her over.

"Put your thumb right here." He indicated the display.

"Wait." She pulled out her cell phone, texted something, and put it back in her purse. She followed his directions, and the lock beeped.

"It's locked. Later, just put your thumb on the display and it will unlock with two beeps."

"Why electronic locks?"

"Easier than combinations, which can be forgotten, and keys that can't be carried in the club." He put his arm around her waist. "Better now?"

"Yes, I don't know what happened, but thank you."

He nodded. "One quick question. Who did you text?"

"Crystal. We developed a code word when out with men. She asked me to text her when I got here and when I got home."

"Good idea." He leaned down and brushed a kiss against her nose. "Let's go before the women coming into the club storm the gates." He picked up the empty glass and guided her out of the facilities and past a line of women.

"Sorry," she said.

A chorus of "no worries" and "no problem," even a few "been there's" were the response.

Max grinned. Most of the members of the club were understanding and willing to help, though there were a few who weren't so willing. He'd have to make sure Sierra stayed clear of them until her confidence was back up to par.

He handed the empty glass to one of the subs standing inside the door of the club. "Please return this to the bar."

"Of course, Master Max." The sub scurried off.

"Welcome to Wicked Sanctuary," Max said.

"The place feels so different," Sierra said.

"What do you mean?"

"I heard the music the night I crashed your party; it had a more primal beat to it. This music is more subdued. And the lighting, I expected darker."

Max laughed. "The music changes. Later tonight, you'll probably hear that primal beat. As for the lighting, we keep it at a good level so everyone can see what is going on. Not so bright that it's distracting, and not so dark that illicit activity will go unnoticed."

Sierra blew out a breath as Jordan walked up to them. "Good evening, Sierra." His gaze went over her body. Max was about to say something, but he noticed Jordan wasn't leering, but he gazed at Sierra in appreciation of what he was seeing. "Max, you're going to need a whip to keep the men away from her."

She stared at Jordan, and he winked. "I've got the Websters settled over by the flogging station. They want to watch a scene there first."

Max nodded. "Fine. I'm going to walk Sierra around to see where she'd like to observe. Where is Damon?"

"By the bondage system."

"Who else do we have here tonight?"

"Zeke and Gabriel are here. Payne said he might show up later."

Max nodded. "Okay, I'll keep an eye out too."

Jordan walked back to the Websters as Max guided Sierra toward the bondage system. He wanted to introduce her to Damon.

****

Sierra reminded herself to breathe as Max took her around the club, showing her all the stations. Some had scenes about to begin; others were empty. Max introduced her to Damon. She remembered him from the night of the private party. Damon smiled and kissed the back of her hand before Max snatched it away.

Max's actions made her giggle and earned her a glare from him, but amusement danced in his eyes as well.

"What would you like to watch first? Remember tonight is all about learning; you don't have to play."

"I'd like to watch the bondage scene." They'd walked by a bondage table, where one of the Doms was setting up a scene with his sub. Sierra was curious about it.

"Good choice." He took her back to that area and helped her onto one of the stools instead of taking a seat on the sofa.

Sierra made sure to keep the skirt covering her private areas as best as she could. Being on a stool, the slits parted, showing off her entire legs and hips. Max moved behind her and placed his hands on her shoulders.

"I want you to watch the sub," he whispered.

Sierra nodded. The sub was a pretty little blonde. What surprised her was that she was dressed a bit more than a lot of people, even more than she was.

Her Dom leaned down and whispered something in her ear, and her cheeks turned red but she nodded.

Slowly, he began unbuttoning the red blouse she wore. As each button came undone, the sub shifted from one foot to the other. She wasn't wearing a bra, so as he drew the shirt off, she was naked on top.

Her hands started to rise, and he grasped her wrists. "Remember, pet." His words were soft, yet Sierra could hear him.

"Sorry, Sir." Her words were just as clear.

Sierra shifted on the stool. To be so exposed in front of people... She couldn't stop her body from trembling and wasn't sure if it was from excitement or fear.

"Look at her. Really look at her," Max whispered in her ear. "Does she appear afraid or uncomfortable?"

Sierra concentrated on the sub's expression and body language. While her cheeks were pink, her shoulders were straight, and she didn't seem uncomfortable.

Her Dom whisked her skirt off, and guided her over to the table. He helped her sit, then he went over to a bag on the floor and pulled out restraints. Sierra saw the woman's breathing increase when he put cuffs on her wrists and ankles, after which, he helped her lie back on the table.

Another tremor hit Sierra. How would it feel to have Max do that to her? Her blood heated and her clit began to throb.

"Now folks, I'm just going to do some simple ties so my pet doesn't slip when I adjust the table, then we'll get down to the fun." The Dom moved quickly, using rope to tie his sub.

"Sir, wouldn't rope burn her skin if she struggles?" Sierra asked Max.

"He's using a hemp rope. Once he raises his sub up, you'll see he didn't tie her wrists or ankles with the rope; he used the rings in the cuffs and the table."

Sierra waited, and the Dom fiddled with something underneath the table. The head of the table began to rise until the table was at a thirty-degree angle. Now she could see. He'd threaded the rope through the rings on the cuffs, and then secured them to rings on the table.

The woman's legs were bent at the knees, while her hands were just slightly above her head.

The Dom picked up more rope. He pressed her left knee down and began tying her leg at the calf, and then the thigh, before doing the same with the right. The way he tied her, her groin area was open to public viewing. Thank goodness she had a thong on or everyone would have been able to see her genitalia. Sierra almost laughed at her use of language.

There was something in the air, a sense of anticipation. The Dom continued to work, and Sierra noted that the sub squirmed once in a while, how flushed her body was, and how rapidly she breathed.

Rope was placed around her midsection. Sierra's stomach clenched. The Dom tied rope above and below her breasts. Sierra squirmed. The sub's breasts were compressed between the strands. That must be painful. Yet she didn't seem to be in pain. Her body looked flushed and relaxed.

And the sub's nipples reacted, becoming taut as she squirmed on the table. The crowd murmured, and the Dom tied off the last rope. "Okay, my pet?"

"Green, Sir."

Club safe words. Green meant the sub was okay. That was the other thing, the entire time the Dom tied her up, he stroked her skin, and he constantly looked at her face. He was paying close attention to her. So the books got that right.

"Now that I have my pet all tied up, we're going to have some fun."

"I thought this was just about bondage?" Sierra asked.

When Max didn't answer, she turned to see him staring at her.

"Oh, sorry, Sir. I thought this was just about bondage, Sir."

Max's lips turned up. "Bondage leads to more fun," he said.

Sierra looked back at the stage. She would have to remember to say Sir. This was so different for her, but to be honest, she didn't mind using Sir or Master in this setting. It felt right.

The Dom returned to the table with something small in his hand. The sub whimpered when she saw it. He caressed her stomach, before slipping his hand beneath her thong.

Sierra let out a gasp as the Dom fingered his sub right there in front of everyone. While technically the observers couldn't see her private...no, her pussy, they could tell what he was doing beneath that thong. Sierra shifted on the stool.

The Dom withdrew his finger. With a smile, he slipped it between his lips and several men let out a moan. The Dom then took the shiny object and pushed it under the thong. Sierra could see his fingers rotating, before he slipped them out.

148

The sub wriggled and looked up at him. He ran his fingers over her face, before holding up a small box and pressing the button. The woman cried out.

"He's put a small vibrating bullet against her clit," Max whispered in her ear.

Sierra's pelvis tightened, and she squeezed her legs together.

"Have you ever played with toys?"

"I tried a vibrator, once, Sir. It didn't do anything for me."

"I see educating you is going to be fun." Max's hands slipped from her shoulders and down her arms. His heat against her almost naked skin made her shiver.

The Dom on the stage leaned over and played with the sub's nipples, and Sierra's eyes widened. They grew bigger as he did so. "Ready for the next part, pet?"

"Green, Sir." Her voice was soft, but Sierra heard something else there. Was it arousal?

She took a deep breath and continued to watch. The Dom pulled two items out of his bag, and went back to the table. Sierra tilted her head as she watched.

"Sir, what does he have there?" She didn't quite understand the round item in the Dom's hand.

"I don't want to spoil it, but you need to know. Those are nipple suckers."

"I don't understand, Sir."

"Just watch."

Sierra shifted on her stool as Max moved his hands to her stomach, lightly caressing her through the lace. She glanced around; no one was paying attention to what he was doing. Good.

The Dom on the stage put the object over the woman's nipples. There was a hose attached and Sierra tilted her head. What the heck? The Dom squeezed the bulb in his hand. He adjusted the objects and squeezed the bulb again.

He nodded and stepped back. The Dom began pumping the bulb. Sierra's eyes grew wide, and her spine stiffened.

"They're nipple pumps." Max traced his fingers over her stomach. "See how her nipples grow. They'll become very sensitive."

"That has to hurt." Her fingers fisted in her lap to prevent herself from covering her own nipples that poked against the lacy fabric. They were in public. Well, sort of.

"Did it hurt when I sucked your nipples?" His fingers slid up to beneath her breasts and Sierra inhaled.

"No, Sir."

"Same concept, except the suction will increase with each pump."

"Yellow, Sir." The sub called out.

The Dom stopped and set the pump on her shoulder. "Very good, pet. You've gone further than we have before."

"He stopped," Sierra panted out. Why was she so out of breath?

"Doms should always respect a sub's safe word. Yellow told him she'd had enough, but not so much to stop the scene. When you've played together a long time you learn each other's pain and pleasure levels."

Sierra jumped when Max cupped her breast, she started to raise her hands. "Hands in your lap, or I'll tie them to the stool." His voice was firm as he spoke in her ear. "Look at the sub's nipples. How hard they are. How dark red they are."

The sub moaned and Sierra squirmed on the stool.

"Easy, Sierra." Max caressed her breasts through the lace. "He's turned on the bullet against her clit. See how her body is flushing, her mouth open as she tries to get more air. Does she appear to be hurting or afraid?"

She looked at the woman. Her body shifted against the table, but her gaze was on her Dom. Sierra let out a gasp at the need and pleasure reflected in the woman's eyes while she stared at her man.

His hand lightly stroked her arm as he spoke to her. Sierra couldn't make out the words, but the woman smiled and nodded.

"No, Sir. She looks…I'm not sure. Happy?" Sierra couldn't come up with the right word. Just then the woman cried out. Sierra jerked against Max.

"He turned up the bullet. Watch her."

Sierra did as Max said. The sub's toes were curling, and she could see her body straining against the restraints. "Please, Sir."

The Dom smiled, picked up the bulb, and gave it a squeeze. The woman screamed, and her head thrashed back and forth. Her climax shook the table as it went on and on. The Dom smiled and flicked the release on the nipple suckers.

He peeled them off her breasts and she let out a moan as he flipped off the bullet.

The audience let out a sigh, a few clapped, and Sierra just stared, dumbfounded. Her body was a quivering mass of want and need.

"Those who clap do it to show appreciation of the sub in letting her Dom take her where he wanted her," Max whispered.

The crowd started to move away, but Max held her there. "See how he's untying her. Each movement includes a caress, and he's talking to her." Sierra kept her eyes on the couple, afraid that people would see Max was playing with her breasts as he spoke. "See how he makes sure she can stand before he moves away to get the blanket."

"What is the blanket for?" She remembered reading something in the romance books about it.

"She's had an emotional high, endorphins are flowing through her system. As she starts to come down from that high, she'll be cold."

The Dom wrapped the sub in the blanket, then picked her up and carried her over to another roped off area, where he set her on the sofa then jumped back to the stage. He quickly put his toys back in his bag and started cleaning.

"I don't understand. What is he doing now, Sir?"

"Basic rules, remember? Clean up the station once you're done."

Sierra nodded. He finished cleaning, put everything back in the supply basket, picked up his bag and returned to the sofa. There, he dropped his bag, sat down and then lifted the sub into his lap.

The woman curled against him, her head on his chest, her eyes closed, but a small smile played on her lips. The woman looked up at her Dom. The love and satisfaction shining in her eyes knocked all of Sierra's preconceived notions out of her head. There was a true connection between the pair.

"Now, he'll give her aftercare, and once she's recovered, they'll either play some more or just watch."

"I..." What could she say? Maybe she wasn't as worldly as she thought.

Max stepped around in front of Sierra. He put his hands on her legs and parted them. Her skirt slipped as Max stepped between them. It still covered her groin, but she felt exposed.

"A true connection between Dom and sub leads to satisfaction, and it is a powerful connection."

Sierra nodded and lowered her gaze. Only to have it snap back to Max's face when he untied her top. He was grinning at her. She started to raise her hands.

"Oh no." He captured them and held them in her lap.

"Max." The halter-top dropped to expose her breasts, the nipples hard and rosy.

"What was that?" His voice went down a notch.

Sierra almost groaned. "Sir."

"Better." He leaned down and licked her right nipple, before doing the same thing to her left.

Her spine stiffened, pushing her breasts forward. He couldn't be doing this. Not here. Not in front of all these people. "Please, Max...Sir. Not in front of everyone."

He lifted his head and grinned down at her. "What people?" She continued to stare at him. "Look around."

She shook her head.

"Look around, Sierra. If you don't, I'll bare your ass and spank it."

She glared at him. "You wouldn't, Sir."

"Spanking is not a hard limit, so yes, I will, if you don't obey me."

When she saw the determination in his eyes, her eyes widened, and she sucked in a breath, turned her head to her right and left, then looked over his shoulder.

"Who is watching?"

"No one, Sir." How was that possible? There had been a lot of people around them. Some of the audience had moved when the scene ended, and some still milled around, but no one was paying them any attention.

"Right. We're not on stage in a scene. We won't gather a crowd unless I want to." He stepped back. "Now, shall we continue your tour?" He put his hands on her waist and lifted her off the stool.

Her knees were weak, but they held her up. She lifted her hands.

"No, my sweet one." He stilled her hands once again. "Leave your top alone."

Sierra fought to breathe. She wanted to argue with him, but then she wanted him to be proud of her. She could do this. A lot of women were naked from the waist up. "Yes, Sir," she whispered.

"That's my girl." He brushed his lips over hers before taking her hand. "Let's keep exploring."

Chapter Eleven

Sierra hid a yawn behind her hand, and Crystal poked her in the side. "Wake up," Crystal whispered.

"I am awake." Sierra shifted on the hard, plastic seat. They were inside Klineman's adult store. Half book shop, half adult shop. Their friend Tessa was giving a talk about erotica and society.

Sierra had been surprised at the number of people here at an eleven o'clock talk on a Sunday morning. Most of the chairs were full. There were at least thirty people in the small room.

Tessa finished and everyone clapped. Sierra and Crystal waited until people finished talking with Tessa before they approached her.

"Great talk," Sierra said.

"I saw you yawning," Tessa said with a grin.

"Not from your talk. Max kept me out late last night."

"Oh yes," Crystal said. "That was a very late *I'm home* text last night. Let's go get lunch, and you can tell us all about it."

Sierra thought about the night before. There was only so much she could say. "Sure, but I want to look around the store a bit."

Tessa and Crystal looked at each other and burst out laughing. "She's finally coming out of her shell," Crystal said.

"Give it a rest."

Her friends always teased her about not being adventurous about her love life or sex. They hadn't grown up with her father and his rules. Interesting. She obeyed Max and his rules, and they didn't scare her or make her cringe. They made her hot.

They walked out of the adult book room. Sierra wanted to laugh. The room was in the back, and a curtain was used to block off the area they used for the books and book club meetings.

The rest of the store was a variety of adult toys, and BDSM-type stuff. Sierra just wanted to look around. Her final class at the club was this coming Thursday. Not that she thought there was much left to go over, but apparently, Max and Jordan did.

Heat filled her. After Saturday night, she wasn't sure about playing at the club. She wasn't an exhibitionist, but after Max freed her breasts, she'd forgotten that she was still uncovered until it was time for them to leave.

It was at that point she realized she'd rarely noticed if the other club members were clothed or not. On occasion, she might notice something. She didn't want to say it was normal because it wasn't. But no one was bothered if others were showing their bodies or not. There were all different body types in the club too.

Sierra wandered up and down the aisles, looking at the toys, restraints, butt plugs, and other various items. While they talked about toys in their class at the club, she wanted a better idea about these items. So, feeling safe with her friends, they wandered through the store.

"Is there anything I can help you with?"

Sierra glanced at the young woman who walked up. Her hair was purple and blue. Sierra smiled. "I'm fine. Just looking."

"No problem. I'm Destiny. If you need anything, let me know." She sauntered away.

Sierra was impressed that there was a woman working here. Actually, she was impressed by the whole place. When Crystal told her they were going to an adult store to hear Tessa talk, Sierra has been skeptical. But the shop was totally different than what she expected.

While the store was at the edge of the city, it had plenty of parking. It was clean and nice looking. There were no back booths or creepy men hanging around. Instead, the small back area held fiction and non-fiction books, as well as the area for meetings.

In the main part of the store were aisles of items that catered to males, females and couples. There was also a freestanding table that held a catalogue with a sign that said, "If we don't have it, we can order it."

There was a clear set of counters at the front, where the cash register sat along with whomever was running the store. Sierra wondered if Destiny worked there or owned the place.

Sierra made her way to the front of the store where her friends stood talking to Destiny.

"All done?" Tessa asked.

"Yep."

"But you're not buying anything," Crystal said.

"Stop it, Crystal." Sierra laughed after she said the words. "I just wanted to look. Thank you, Destiny." She opened the door and walked out.

A small breeze caressed her skin, reminding her of Max's light touch on her body last night. Heat flowed through her veins. Oh man, she had it bad.

"I believe you mentioned lunch," she said to Crystal.

"The pub is open, let's go grab a burger and talk."

* * * *

Max went over the books for the club one more time. They were doing quite well. Between membership fees and the private parties, they were more than meeting expenses. He pulled up his calendar.

They had one private party coming up. Thanksgiving was around the corner, and then the Christmas holiday would be upon them. He'd have to talk to Jordan and Damon and see if they wanted to do a New Year's Eve party. Max sat back in his chair. He hadn't really thought about the holidays, outside of watching football.

Maybe because, when he was married, his ex always wanted to make a big production out of the holidays, then got all upset when her plans didn't work out. Max shook his head. Yeah, he was a typical guy, but his family was out of state. Actually, he looked at the calendar again. His parents were going on a two-month cruise next week, and his brother was still overseas somewhere serving in the military.

Family get-togethers had been few and far between in the last few years, mainly due to his father being semi-retired now. His mother loved having him around, and they traveled and enjoyed themselves. That made Max happy.

His brother loved the military. He kept saying he was a career man, but sometimes Max wondered. His brother continued to advance in rank, but there were assignments he would have preferred to avoid and was not permitted to talk about.

Max made sure the private parties were synced up with the club's electronic calendar. He closed the spreadsheet he was working on and made a note to pay quarterly taxes next month.

He sat back in his chair and pulled out Sierra's folder. Her last class was this Thursday night. The new members with their mentor would go over the checklist to see if there were any changes. He'd been pleased with her and the way she'd handled the club last night.

There were some things she'd shied away from. He looked through her list. Yes, most of those were listed as her hard limits. He flipped the pages. She'd put bondage as a soft limit, along with toys, restraints, and flogging.

He filed those away. He went down the list until he found what he was looking for. Nudity in public, she'd put down as unsure. He'd talk with her about that. Last night, she'd done quite well with having her breasts exposed. One day, he'd get her totally exposed in the club, if she agreed; right now, he wanted her to get used to it…and him. His cock twitched. Max put the file back away, and picked up his tablet before going into the family room.

He turned on the football game and sat down. He pulled up the website he wanted, and did a search for two books. He ordered them and had them delivered to Sierra. He'd text her later to expect them.

* * * *

Thursday came way too fast for Sierra, but in a way, she was ready. Max had texted her every day. Sunday to tell her he'd ordered some books for her. Then on Monday to ask her if the books arrived. They had.

Tuesday and Wednesday were more just check-in texts, asking how her day went and if she was missing him. She laughed at the last, but she had missed him. Missed his touch, the sound of his voice, heck, just having him around. It was funny how he'd wormed his way into her heart so quickly.

Of course the two books he sent her hadn't helped. How the hell did he know about erotic romance? He'd sent her two books by two different authors. Authors Tessa talked about all the time, but Sierra hadn't read yet.

Sierra had stayed up late Tuesday and Wednesday nights reading. Not that she hadn't read erotic romance before, but these were different. Well the books weren't different, she was. Her mind was wide open to the possibilities kink could bring into her life.

She parked her car in the club lot and walked inside. Ralph sat behind the desk as usual. After Sierra signed in, she went back to the classroom. Max and Jordan were already there.

"Evening, Sierra," Jordan said.

"Master Jordan." She was getting better at remembering titles.

"Not in the classroom," he said, then looked at Max. "I'll leave you two alone." And he left.

"Are the Websters not coming?" The couple had seemed in their element last weekend.

"Jordan's meeting them inside the club." He gestured to the chair, and Sierra sat down. Max sat next to her and put a folder, along with a pen and pad of paper, down. "They'll go over their stuff in there."

Sierra swallowed. "I know tonight is our last class."

"Yes. It's a good time to go over your limits and see what's changed now that you've experienced the club." He opened the folder. "I added some notes to them from what I saw last Saturday night with you. Look at them and tell me if I'm wrong."

Sierra picked up the form and started going through it. He'd noted a few things on her soft limits, all of which were good with her. He hadn't touched the hard limits at all. She stopped at nudity in the club – he changed that to a soft limit. Her face grew warm.

"You're hesitating. Am I wrong about nudity?"

"I don't know." She didn't. Once she got over the fact that her breasts were hanging out where anyone could see, it didn't bother her, but being totally nude?

Max covered her hand with his. "Do you trust me, Sierra?"

"Yes." She did. They may not have known each other long, but she did trust him. He'd seen her fall apart and hadn't run or belittled her.

"Good. I won't push you into accepting anything you don't want, and I will go slowly. Remember you can always use your safe words."

She took a deep breath. He was right, she could. "All right." She looked over the last couple of pages. "All is good." She put the pages back into the folder and handed it to him before her nerves got the best of her.

Max stared at her. "That isn't totally convincing me."

"I'm still nervous, but I want to try."

"That's all I ask. Let's talk about what you want to do in the club and what nights you'd like to attend."

"Depending on the week, Fridays and Saturdays are probably the best since I don't work weekends."

He nodded. "I want you to think about this, but I'd like us to play at the club this weekend. You get to pick the night and what you'd like to try."

Now came the hard part: what did she want to try? Sierra closed her eyes and a scene from one of the books she read flashed in her memory. Her body grew hot.

"Whatever you're thinking, I approve."

"What?" She opened her eyes.

"Your skin flushed, and your breathing increased, so whatever you were thinking aroused you."

Damn if he wasn't right.

"Tell me what you were thinking?"

Open and frank communication, wasn't that what he'd told her in one of their classes when they went over the rules and other information about the club and the lifestyle. "I want to be tied up." Her voice was soft.

"I can do that." He reached out and brushed his fingers over her cheek. "What else?"

Their gazes met. "Toys," she whispered. "I want to understand the appeal, like the bullet."

"That seems reasonable." He ran his other hand between her breasts.

"I saw some nipple clamps at the adult store on Sunday. I want to try them, but some of them look painful." Her nipples hurt as she remembered the set that had what looked like metal teeth.

"You were at the adult store?"

"Ummm, yeah." She didn't need to be embarrassed; this was Max. "Tessa was giving a talk there, so Crystal and I went. Afterward, I looked around."

"I'm glad you were being proactive."

"Yeah, well, I saw all sorts of things."

"I bet." He let out a chuckle. "I'll start you off with nipple clamps that look like tweezers. Did you see those?"

"Yes, I did."

"Those are very adjustable and the perfect place to start."

"Okay."

"You do realize you'll be naked from the waist up for the nipple clamps."

"Yes, but for the bullet, can you do like the Dom did on Saturday night?"

"Leave you in a thong?"

She nodded. She wouldn't be totally naked then.

"I can, or you can wear the skirt, and I'll make sure the fabric covers your pussy."

She hadn't thought of that.

"I do want you to realize, I will be touching you a lot in the club."

"I figured that." He'd kept his hands on her Saturday night. Who was she kidding? Max liked to touch, and she loved his hands on her body.

"Let me be clear. I will touch you wherever I want, your breasts, your pussy, your ass, anywhere on your body."

This time the heat flooded her entire body just thinking about his hands on her in the places he mentioned.

"I'm going to be your Dom and your teacher, if you'll allow me."

Her insides quivered, and a sense of ease flowed through her. "I can't think of anyone else I could do this with." It was the truth. She trusted Max.

"Good. We've gone over the rules and protocols of the club, but I'd like to discuss my expectations."

Sierra swallowed. She had never been good at living up to someone else's expectations.

"I already see the apprehension in your eyes. What's going on there?" He took her hand in his. His warmth seeped into her bones.

"I..." She shook her head. Talking about her father was never easy for her. She'd buried so much of it away. *Buck-up, buttercup. You tamed those demons a long time ago.* It wasn't like her father was even in the same state as she was. Hell, she hadn't even talked to him in years, not after their last conversation where he'd called her a whore. "I could never live up to my father's expectations," she whispered.

"Sometimes parents have unrealistic aspirations" He caressed her skin, keeping her grounded.

"True." Sierra swallowed and raised her gaze to meet his. "I moved out when I was eighteen and never looked back. My father was strict, so strict that if I put a toe out of line he'd whip me with a belt." Her skin tightened and her breathing increased. She hated that her father could still affect her.

Max stiffened, his eyes growing dark. "Bastard."

Sierra wanted to agree but her throat dried up at the look in Max's eyes. It wasn't one of pity; it was one of anger. He was on her side.

"Sweetheart, my expectations are that, in the club, you will obey me. I will push some of your boundaries, but that's why we have safe words. I would never beat you with a belt or anything that harsh. I don't believe in pain for the sake of pain."

Her breath rushed out of her. "I would never ask for pain. For obvious reasons, I'm not sure about flogging." At least her voice was steady. She was worried he would notice the anxiety she was trying so hard to hide.

164

"That makes sense. When we get to that point, I'll start off with little stuff. I can tell you I have never been into pain, even when a sub wants it. It gives me no pleasure, so I'm no sadist."

"But some members are." She remembered some of the things she had seen on Saturday night.

"Yes, they use whips and canes, but their subs enjoy it as well or it wouldn't be happening. Remember, everything done in the club is consensual. If anyone does anything that isn't, then we intervene."

"That seems fair."

"Okay with my expectations then?"

"Only in the club?" She wanted to make sure she had her head fully around this.

"The club and my bedroom."

A smile curved her lips. "Leave you to slip that in there. Yes, I'm good."

"Any other questions?"

"One more." Sierra bit her lip. How did she ask this one?

"What is it? You're thinking awfully hard."

"You don't..." She took a deep breath. "You aren't going to share me with others, right?" Sierra ducked her head.

"I prefer to keep you to myself. If you want a threesome or to explore with a woman, I can arrange it. But I don't remember you putting that on your list."

"No." She shook her head and breathed out a sigh of relief. "No more questions right now."

"All right, that's it. Classes are done."

"That's it?" Why was she surprised? The Thursday night classes weren't really as hard as she thought they'd be.

"Yes. Knowing the basics is good, but you have to experience it." He drew her to her feet. "Saturday we will play. Shall I send another outfit over to you or do you want to wear the skirt?"

"I'm not sure." The outfit she had would work well, but then she'd already worn it once. Would anyone notice if she wore it a second time?

"I'll send you another outfit; you make the decision on which one you want to wear. Be here at eight."

"You're letting me drive myself?" That threw her. He'd insisted on picking her up the other night.

"Yes, as much as I want to pick you up, Saturday will be busy. There's a private party in the club Friday night, so the next day is always a little more hectic."

"Not the group that was here before?" She shivered.

"No, Cook and his group will never set foot in my club again, and I've put the word out."

"There are other private clubs?" Why did she feel like she'd been living under a rock?

"A few, but not many in the area. We have a private forum we use to discuss problem members, and that helps all of us keep our clubs safe, sane, and consensual."

"Was the Saints and Sinners party private?" She remembered the music and the number of cars.

"No, that was a club event. Tomorrow night is for a large swingers group. They're coming in from all over."

Her eyes went wide. "Swingers."

"The club caters to everyone. They follow the same rules as the rest of us. It just makes for a long night for Jordan, Damon and myself, plus some of the other dungeon monitors we have."

Sierra swallowed. "Ummm...You don't expect me to play with others, do you?"

Max laughed. "No, sweetheart." He ran his finger over her hot cheek. "I'm very possessive of you. I don' share."

"I noticed that. I don't remember seeing anything about the colored wrist bands."

"Ah those. Yes, it's something new. We haven' added it to the rules yet." He lifted her hand and drew his fingers around her wrist. "We've been trying to figure ou a way for people to recognize certain things withou having to ask the same questions over and over."

Sierra tilted her head. "Explain, please."

"We discovered over the last year that some Doms weren't sure how experienced a few of the subs were, and they'd spend a lot of time trying to find one to suit their needs. Same with the subs."

"I had a white band."

"Yes, you'll have a white one for a while, but it will be clear that you belong to me. White is for a new member with little experience."

"You wore a black one."

"Black is for Masters of the club, those of us who have been granted that status. Black and yellow is for Master and dungeon monitor. You'll see some DMs with just yellow."

"Interesting. What other colors?" This was fascinating. She knew there were different levels of play, but the way Max and his friends had decided to do the wrist bands would help identify someone easier.

"Red is a sadist, red and white is a masochist. Purple and white means the sub is taken. Pink and white means the sub has medium experience. Green and white means the sub is experienced."

"And the Doms?"

"Only the Masters and DMs wear anything."

"Seems a little one sided."

Max wrinkled his nose. "Maybe, but we really don't get very many inexperienced Doms."

"Why not?"

"You're really interested?"

"Yes."

"Okay, let's say a single guy survived the first night and all the classes up until now. He would have another four weeks of classes working with one of the Masters in the club to get his experience level up from a novice if he knew nothing. There are a series of tests for him to complete."

"What happens if he fails?"

"Depends on the degree of failure." He rubbed his finger over her nose. "I'm not going to tell you everything, but we screen very carefully."

"Even the subs?"

"Yes. While the class is only four weeks, the Dom instructor responsible for his sub, he watches and evaluates the student every time he or she are in the club. If there's an issue, it's talked out between Dom and student."

"I see. Have subs failed?" She wasn't sure she liked this evaluation stuff, but in a way, it made sure people were doing this because they wanted to.

"Yes. Some think they really want this lifestyle, but as they progress with our classes, they back out or just aren't suitable. Look at how the first night went."

"I thought it was odd we lost so many people."

"That was unusual. I suspect the single guy had something in his background check he didn't want anyone to know about. The two women, I think, were more interested in having fun than wanting to learn. And the couple...they were harder to read, I suspect they were hoping for more bedroom play than the club."

"Makes sense. What about the couple with Jordan?"

"They're a little more experienced than most." He rose to his feet, pulling her with him. "Time for you to go home and get some sleep, I know you have work tomorrow."

"Yeah." Sierra didn't want to leave, but he was right. She did have work to do. She paused at her car.

Max cupped her chin, and his lips covered hers. Sierra didn't even hesitate, she kissed him back, enjoying the feel of his mouth against hers, the way his tongue tangled with hers.

"Can you do an early dinner tomorrow?" he asked, slightly breathless from their kiss.

"I can."

"Good. I'll pick you up at your apartment at four-thirty, we'll have dinner, then I'll take you home before I have to be here at the club at seven."

Pleasure swept through her with the idea of going to dinner with him. "Max, I appreciate you teaching me. I don't think another man would be as patient."

He frowned, then his face lightened. "From the moment I saw you, I knew you were mine to teach. I wouldn't have it any other way, sweetheart."

Chapter Twelve

Sierra rushed in the door of her apartment at four. Max would be here in thirty minutes. She dropped her purse on the table and ran for her bedroom. Why, today of all days, did she have to end up on a conference call that ran overtime.

In record time, she'd showered, redone her makeup, and dressed. She ran her hands down the fabric of her top. She always liked this cashmere sweater she'd gotten on sale a few years ago.

The doorbell rang, and she checked to see who it was before opening it.

"Hello Max."

"Hi." He drew her into his embrace and brushed his lips across hers. "Ready?"

"Let me grab my purse." He loosened his hold. Sierra turned and grabbed her purse off the table. Once she'd locked the door, they were off.

"Where are we having dinner?" she asked as Max pulled out of his parking spot.

"I thought we'd go to the steak and seafood place down by the inlet. We can have a nice view while we have dinner."

"Sounds good." There were several restaurants at the inlet. She'd never been to any of them, only to the farmers market nearby. "How was your day?"

"Slow. What about you?"

"Busy. I was afraid I was going to be late for our date. But I made it."

"So I see." He flashed a grin and her breath caught in her throat.

"Can I ask you a question? You told me tonight's private party is a swinger group. Can you tell me more?" She knew what swingers were. Spouse-swapping is what she was thinking, but how did they come to be a part of the BDSM scene? She was curious.

"I'm not sure that's such a good idea." He maneuvered around a slow moving car. Sierra realized how relaxed she was with Max driving. With Carl's assault on the road and drivers, she'd been tense and holding on to the door. The difference between confidence and aggression.

"Why?" Sierra frowned. "Oh wait, if you can't talk about it, it's okay."

"You're a member of the club so talking to you isn't the issue." He glanced at her then back to the road. "I don't want to frighten you."

"Frighten..." The lights came on in her brain. No, she wasn't experienced. "I thought swingers just shared partners?"

"That's part of it." He reached over and took her hand from where it rested on her leg. "Some enjoy BDSM, some heavier than others. It's one of the reasons I'm working tonight. I need to monitor the group."

"When you say heavy you mean S & M?" A shiver racked her body.

"Yes, plus there will be foursomes and more."

"Okay, then." This was unexpected. Her mind was spinning with the information.

"Very few people like all types of BDSM. We have a saying that goes like this: your kink is not my kink, and that's okay."

"I can say that fits this situation for me." She wasn't into the heavier BDSM scene. She enjoyed what Max had done to her so far.

Max pulled into a parking spot, and they strolled from his vehicle to the restaurant. The outside was painted white and blue with tile that created an ocean wave. Max held the glass door open for her.

The interior of light wood paneling and a gas fireplace gave the restaurant a cozy feel. The lobby area was full of people.

"Mr. Preston, so nice to see you again," the maître d' said. "I have your table ready. Please follow me."

"Thank you." Max gestured for her to go ahead of him.

The eyes of the not-yet-seated people drilled into her back. She felt bad for them and tugged at Max's hand. He glanced at her, and she tilted her head.

"We have a reservation."

"I see." When he gestured for her to continue to their seat, she released his hand. They were led to the only empty table, an intimate table for two with a view of the inlet and the marina.

"Your waiter will be right here." The maître d' said before he left them alone.

"So, you planned to come here tonight?" Sierra asked as she picked up her menu.

"I made a reservation for us, yes. This way we got a table with a view and didn't have to wait."

Sierra glanced at the menu. So many choices. A sigh left her lips as she read the selections. It had been a long day, and she didn't want to make another decision. Sierra folded her menu and placed her hands on top of it. "Will you choose for me?" How would he react to her question?

Max's eyes widened. She stifled a smile, amazed she could surprise him. That was good.

"I can. Anything you won't eat?"

"No clams, anchovies, or mushrooms. Everything else is okay."

"All right." He glanced at the menu and shut it as the waitress walked up. "We're going to start with Caesar salad, no anchovies, the filet mignon both medium but not super pink, baked potato, one with everything and one with butter and bacon, house vegetables for two. We'll need one dessert of the day at the end of the meal."

"Very good choices. To drink?"

Max looked at her. "Water is fine," Sierra said.

"Same for me."

"Thank you. I'll be back with bread, butter and your salads."

"So tell me about your busy day."

It took a minute for her brain to catch up with Max's question. He knew her better than she thought. And that didn't seem like a bad thing at all.

Dinner conversation flowed around their days and other mundane things. Sierra was kind of surprised. Not only were they talking about mundane things, but she was totally relaxed. Max did that to her. He got beneath her defenses. It should worry her, but it didn't. She was willing to go with the flow.

"Will you tell me about your childhood?" Max asked after dessert was delivered.

The fork in Sierra's hand froze on the way to her mouth. He was asking, not demanding to know more about her childhood. She slipped the fork into her mouth and chewed her food while she thought about his request.

It was something he needed to know, at least some of it. "This isn't an easy subject for me to talk about."

"I understand. How about this: What do you want to know about me?"

"Everything." The word slipped out, and it was the truth. She really did want to know more about him.

"Fair enough. Let's see. I have a younger brother who is currently serving in the military, and my parents are more or less retired and on a cruise right now."

"That's nice. Do they know about the club?"

"Yes, and no. They are aware I own a club, but not what goes on inside the club."

"All right. What about serious relationships?" She stiffened after she asked the question, but then took a deep breath and forced herself to relax. This was probably something she should have asked before now.

"A few relationships. As for serious, I would say only one." His face turned serious. "I'm divorced." He waved his hand in the air. "I'm not proud of it."

Sierra blinked several times. That had surprised her. Why would anyone divorce Max? Maybe he divorced her? "May I ask what happened?"

He nodded. "In the beginning, things were okay. My ex was not into kink, and I had her permission to indulge—her word not mine—my kink as long as there was no sex involved."

"You mentioned you met Jordan and Damon at a munch." This was interesting. He must have loved his wife a lot to marry someone not interested in kink.

"Yes. Because my wife wasn't into kink, I sought out a kink partner. Jordan, Damon and I hit it off and became friends. They were not looking for sex, but a real relationship with a sub."

Sierra nodded. She could see that. "Why did you get a divorce?"

"How do you know I asked for it?"

Sierra laughed. "Because you wouldn't stay in a marriage that wasn't working."

"True." He glanced out the window and then back to her. "As much as my ex said she was fine with me getting my kink in other places, she wasn't. She began to whine and cry whenever I wanted to go out. It drove me crazy until I finally confronted her. That's when it came out she couldn't stand that I was into kink. Those words ended my marriage. She lied to me, and I won't stand for that."

"She was bitter you had a life you enjoyed?"

"In some ways, yes, though she got everything she wanted in the divorce. We had a pre-nup, so the house and land where the club is was safe. I made sure of that."

"And she just disappeared."

"Yep, she did. And I was happy she was out of my life."

"So no one after her?"

He paused and Sierra waited. There was something there.

"One person." He was silent as he gazed out the window at the marina. When he turned back to her, his eyes were sad and his face lined. "Right after I opened the club, I started training a sub."

"Like you're training me?" A burning sensation started in her stomach. She had no reason to feel jealous, but she did.

"In some ways, yes." He reached across the table and laid his hand on hers. "To set your mind at ease, this sub was never in my home, nor did I want a relationship outside the club with her like I do with you."

"I see." Did she? From everything she knew about him, he worked hard to keep his life compartmentalized, keep the club separate from his everyday life. "I'm guessing it didn't work."

"Spectacular failure." He rubbed his fingers against the back of her hand.

"Will you tell me?"

"I don't want to scare you."

Sierra stared at him and took a deep breath. Jump or run. She was willing to jump. "I'm not a porcelain doll, Max. You'll understand about that soon. I can handle it."

He paused, squeezed her fingers and then let out a breath. "The sub was fairly new to the lifestyle, not as new as you were. She had some experience, and I'd seen her at some of the parties I'd attended. So, when she asked about becoming part of the club, I didn't see anything wrong with it." He let out a sigh. "Back then I didn't do as much due diligence as I do now."

"Oh?" That was surprising.

"We didn't do background checks; we trusted people. We started them about three years ago, and the classes you've taken only right after that."

"I'm guessing there was something in her background."

"Yes. She hid it well. I began to train and play with her in the club. What I didn't know was that, not only was she seeing another Dom outside the club, which was acceptable, but that Dom was also her dealer."

"Drugs." That's how Max recognized Carl was under the influence.

"Yes. Cocaine, hard core. As I said, I didn't know until one night at the club. We were getting ready to scene, but I noticed something was off. She wasn't acting right. Her breathing was too choppy and she was anxious over a scene we'd done before."

"She was high."

"More than that. She had overdosed, but I didn't know it at the time. I took her aside and told her we weren't going to scene. She started ranting at me. Jordan came over to help, but she wouldn't stop. Her breathing got worse and worse even as we tried to calm her down." He drew his hand back and ran it over his face. "I never want to see anything like that again."

"I'm so sorry, Max." Sierra reached out to him, cradling his free hand in hers, holding it tight.

"She had a seizure right there in the club. Luckily a member was a doctor. He rushed over while Jordan called 911. It was over within minutes. She died."

Sierra's breath caught in her throat. "You felt responsible." Of course he would. The woman had been his sub, someone he took care of.

"Yes. Why hadn't I seen it before? Let alone why would she do that to herself. I just didn't understand. And I failed because of that."

"Oh Max." She squeezed his hand. "I have no idea why people use drugs. But it wasn't your fault, just like it isn't my fault about Carl."

177

"I was her Dom."

"And she wasn't honest with you. How did you find out about the Dom who was also her dealer?"

"After emergency personnel and the police arrived, her phone started ringing. At that time, we just had cubby holes for personal belongings. One of the other subs brought her things to the police. The police officer answered the phone."

Sierra frowned. If the police answered the phone... "He came to the club?"

Max shook his head. "No. They told him not to. I wasn't sure if there was anyone to take care of the funeral or anything else. So I looked up her emergency contact."

"It was him."

"Yes." The lines on his face deepened. "The man was not only her Dom and dealer but also her husband."

"She lied."

"Big time. I saw him at the funeral. He didn't want me there, but I didn't give a damn. I stood in back, away from everyone to keep from flaying him alive. The second the funeral was over he was arrested and charged."

"Oh Max. I'm so sorry. Two women who lied to you." That had to be hard on a man with his integrity.

"Since then, I've run the club but left the training of subs to others. I didn't trust my judgment."

"Why me?" While she hadn't lied to him, she hadn't told him everything. She needed to tell him. He was bearing his soul to her.

"Honestly, there was a spark in you that called to me. Wet, cold, and standing on my doorstep, eyes wide at how I was dressed, yet polite and worried about interrupting a party. You found a crack in my armor that night and I found I couldn't let you go."

Sierra smiled. "You wormed your way into my life, too."

"I did." His lips tilted up.

"My mother died when I was twelve." Sierra said the words quickly in the hopes that the pain would pass fast. It didn't. Her heart clenched in her chest, but she knew she had to get through this.

This time, Max's hand squeezed hers.

"I didn't realize how much of a buffer she was between my father and me. He wasn't a happy man, and when mom passed, he got worse. He wanted me to do everything around the house, keep it clean, cook, plus go to school and keep my schoolwork up. Lord forbid if my grades dropped."

"But there is more."

She nodded and swallowed, trying to get the lump in her throat to release. "When I turned fifteen my father changed even further. He hated everything I wore. Boys were evil. I was lying all the time." Sierra closed her eyes and swallowed. "He beat me."

The words were soft. A tremor went though her body. Max stiffened and then pushed his chair back. He rose. Sierra put her hands up and motioned for him to stop. He stared at her. "Please, Max." He sat.

"Sweetheart." His voice was tender and calm. Yet she could see the anger vibrating off him.

"That's why I'm not sure about flogging. While you say it's sensual, I'm just not sure."

"Has watching the flogging at the club bothered you?"

"Yes and no, mostly because I hear your voice in my head saying to watch the sub, who isn't screaming in pain but in pleasure. Even Regina told me flogging can be a wonderful release. She said that a lot of what she does in the club is to let go after being a nurse all day and controlling her emotions."

"That's how many feel. We don't have many masochists in the club. We do have them, but they're few and far between."

Sierra nodded. "My father was a hard man, and he didn't understand why I left as soon as I could."

"How did you leave?"

"His ideas that I had to be a straight A student backfired on him. Because I did so well, I began receiving scholarships for college. My father couldn't turn down free education. So off to college I went, and there, I was finally out from underneath him. He couldn't do anything when I wouldn't come home. He couldn't touch my scholarships."

"What did you major in?"

She was relieved he changed the subject. "I actually had a double major economics and psychology."

Max whistled. "Those are heavy subjects."

"Yeah. What about you? College degree?"

Max laughed. "Computer sciences, if you haven't guessed that already, and business."

"You're no slouch yourself."

Max laughed and glanced at his watch. "I hate to cut this short but I need to get to the club."

"I'm glad we talked, even if the subject wasn't the best," Sierra said standing up. And she did. She really did. Her upbringing wasn't something she talked about. Ever. This, telling Max, well, it lifted a weight from her shoulders she didn't realize she was carrying. She smiled up at him.

"Me too." Putting his arm around her waist, he guided her out to his vehicle. "Because I can't wait to play with you and show you just how sensual my attention, in any way, can feel."

Pleasure hit her low in her belly. She couldn't wait either.

* * * *

Sierra pulled into a parking spot on Saturday evening, her heart pounding. Why wasn't this getting any easier? Maybe because the man waiting for her set her blood on fire?

After dinner last night, she'd done a lot of thinking. She was glad they talked. The more they talked, the closer Sierra became to Max. He'd become important in her life in the short time they'd known each other.

Before he had to get to the club, he'd taken her to her apartment, and like randy teenagers, they made out on her sofa. Max wasn't pushing her, but her body was demanding satisfaction in a way it never had before.

Hell, she allowed Max liberties with her body that she'd never let another man have. Anticipation and nervousness flowed through her as she walked to the door of Wicked Sanctuary. She paused and ran her fingers over the smooth wooden letters, WS, on the door.

Taking a deep breath, she stepped inside. Max waited by the reception desk for her. Sierra signed in and got her wristband. Purple and white this time. Max had on a black and yellow.

"You're a monitor tonight?"

"Yeah, we're a little short-handed for the first few hours. One of the other Doms will cover after he finishes a scene with his sub." He drew her to him. "But no worries; tonight we play."

A shiver slid down her spine, excitement and trepidation mingled together. "Sounds like a plan."

"Go put your stuff in a locker. I'll be waiting."

"Yes, Sir." Sierra walked into the ladies' area. Regina and Samantha were both there.

"Hey Sierra," Regina said.

"Hi Regina, Samantha." Samantha just glared at her with those cold blue eyes. Sierra wondered what she'd done to Samantha to make her glare like that.

Sierra found a locker, took off her jacket and her shoes, put her purse in the locker, and then closed and locked it. Tonight's outfit was a little more daring. When the box arrived this afternoon, she was apprehensive at first, but once she tried it on, she realized Max knew what he was doing.

The deep blue baby doll type top was held together by ties over her shoulders and at the sides. The thong was a little uncomfortable, but Max had sent her a wide lace one in the same color as the top. It covered her lady bits quite well.

If she was honest, the thong only showed off a little more of her ass than at the beach. The baby doll top, while she could see the outline of her breasts and skin, didn't completely expose her unless it was untied.

She decided to go without high-heeled shoes. She agreed with Regina they would kill a person after a while, and Sierra had discovered on her last visit it was easier for her to move around without anything on her feet. That was something she forgot to ask Max about. The floor in the club, while it looked like dark hardwood, had a cushion to it.

"I'm surprised you showed back up," Samantha said.

Sierra turned and looked at the blonde. "Oh? Why is that?"

Samantha flicked the blue ribbon on Sierra's shoulder. "How could he like a bit of fluff like you?" She circled Sierra, who had to steel herself from stepping back and away from the woman.

"Master Max is only playing with you, you know," Samantha said. "Everyone knows. There's no way you could hold his attention."

Regina let out a gasp. "Samantha, that's uncalled for."

"I'm not about to let this novice take my place. Max is mine."

Sierra's stomach tightened. Was this truly what Max wanted? She didn't think so. Still, she refused to show the sub how her words stung. "Really Samantha? Because I haven't seen Max throw even an iota of interest in your direction."

"You bitch." Samantha took a step forward.

"Enough." Regina stepped in front of Samantha.

Samantha glared at Regina and raised her hand, ready to swing.

"No, you don't." There was no way Sierra was going to allow this woman to hit Regina.

Sierra pulled Regina out of the way and snapped her arm up to block Samantha's blow.

Samantha let out a snarl as Sierra blocked her left arm, but missed her right hand. Samantha slapped Sierra across the face.

Regina let out a gasp and ran from the room. Samantha cackled with satisfaction. Rules. The club followed rules. As much as she wanted a physical heart-to-heart with Samantha, Sierra reminded herself that violence wasn't the answer. She drew herself up to her full height, her cheek throbbing.

"I believe you just violated several rules, Samantha."

Something flashed in the woman's eyes, then she shook her head. "No one saw."

"Oh, but someone did." Max's voice was low and tight as he crossed the room with Regina, Jordan hot on his tail. Max took Sierra's chin in his hand and turned her head.

His features tightened. Sierra placed her hand over his. "I'm okay."

"She hit you." Max's expression was now thunderous.

"Just a sting, nothing more." Her arm hurt more than her cheek.

"She's lying," Samantha said. "I didn't hit her."

"You will not speak until spoken to; is that clear?" Jordan said, his tone harsh. Samantha shut her mouth.

"I'm sorry, Master Max. Sierra was protecting me and pulled me out of the way when Samantha was going to hit me," Regina said from behind Max.

"You did the right thing in coming to get us, Regina." Max released Sierra and turned to Samantha. "You're suspended from the club until after the New Year, and then you will attend class to remind you of the rules. Lastly, if you choose to return to the club, you will make a public apology to each and every Master/Dom present, plus Sierra and Regina."

Samantha started to protest, but Max held up his hand. "I'm being lenient in this case, and you know it. You are never to put your hands on another sub or club member without permission." Max turned to Jordan. "Escort her to her car and make sure she leaves."

"Will do, Max."

Max turned back to Sierra, took her hand in his, and led her into the club. He didn't speak as he guided her to one of the sofas, sat, and pulled her onto his lap. "You didn't retaliate."

Sierra sighed. "No, I don't like violence. Also, knowing the club rules, I didn't want to ruin our first night playing."

"I don't know if I could have been as kind."

"Was what you did lenient?"

"Yes, Samantha has been a member since right after we opened. We had an incident a few months ago where a sub struck another one. That sub is no longer a member, but not only that, she was punished by every Dom in the club that night."

"They didn't hurt her?" Sierra's voice was soft.

"No. It was her choice of punishment. Basically the Doms tormented her to the brink of climax and then wouldn't let her orgasm. It went on for several hours, then she was escorted off the property and told never to return."

"Poor thing."

"I don't tolerate violence in my club. There are limits for a reason."

Sierra nodded. Her arm still stung, she lifted it to see a red spot. "You're hurt." Max gently took her arm.

"Samantha packs a wallop." She smiled at Max who was frowning. "I'm okay, Max." She put her hand on his cheek. "Don't let this ruin our night."

"We are in the club."

"Yes, Sir, or should I call you Master?"

For a moment, Sierra wasn't sure if Max would let go of his anger, but then he grinned.

"Either is fine. So are you ready to do a scene together?"

"Yes, Master." She liked the way that rolled off her tongue.

He cupped her face and kissed her with such sweetness, her heart melted. Pulling back, he tipped her head up. "Trust me?"

"Yes, Master," she whispered without hesitation.

"All right, my sweet." He brushed his lips over hers again as if he couldn't get enough of her. "Let's go to the bondage area. I think I have the perfect place to restrain you."

Sierra slipped off his lap with a shiver. She wanted to do this, she reminded herself. Max led her over to the bondage area and then up onto the small raised stage. A chair was positioned in the middle.

That is, if you could call it a chair. The seat was raised off the floor, so anyone sitting wouldn't be able to touch the ground. There was a crossbar made of wood and covered in leather padding. Eyebolts were screwed into the top of the bar. A shiver skittered along her spine. A large pillow lay next to the chair.

"Kneel on the pillow." Max told her.

Sierra took a deep breath and did as he instructed. They'd talked about this. She would kneel and wait for him to get everything ready. She watched him pull items out of his bag and place them on the small table.

He walked over to her with a pair of wrist cuffs made of black and red leather, lined with fleece. He calmly buckled them on her wrists, making sure there was plenty of room to avoid impeding circulation in her wrists and hands.

His fingers went to the ties on her baby doll top. "Ready?"

"Yes, Master. I'm green." A shiver of excitement shot from her nipples to her clit as he untied the first one on her right shoulder, then the one on her left. The top sagged. Max then undid the side ties, and removed the garment.

She glanced around the play area. People were starting to mill around. Her stomach clenched.

"Eyes on me, sub." Her gaze went to his face. "Keep your eyes on me. No one else exists but us."

"Yes, Master."

He helped her to her feet and led her over to the chair. Max turned her so she was facing him, then he grasped her by the waist and lifted her. Instinctively her hands went to his shoulders.

"Easy." He placed her in the seat. Her legs were parted, but not widely. "Don't move." He snagged another set of restraints that matched the ones on her wrists and placed them on her ankles. Next, he picked up a bunch of double-ended metal clips.

He knelt and attached her left ankle first before doing her right. While it wasn't tight, she wouldn't be able to move far. Max stood and took her right arm, straightened it and used one of the clips to attach her wrist to the crossbeam, then did the same with the left arm.

"Okay?"

"Green, Master." She was. Anticipation fizzed through her body.

His hazel eyes grew brighter each time she addressed him as Master. Max went back to the table, grabbed a couple of other things, and put them in the pocket of his pants. She hoped one was the bullet vibrator. Sierra kept her gaze on him. Her body was hot. She wiggled her ass.

Max noticed and gave her a sexy grin. "Can't wait to start, sub?"

"Anticipation is hard, Master."

"Yes, it is."

Sierra glanced at his crotch. His cock was hard and pressing against the fabric of his pants. Oh my goodness, she did that? She barely prevented a giggle from escaping her mouth. Somehow she didn't think Max would approve.

He ran his fingers over her left breast, bringing her attention back to his face. Her nipples were already hard. "Let's see how hard I can make these." He rolled them between his fingers, and Sierra let out a little groan. Her breasts had become so sensitive since he started playing with them. Her nipples hardened into tight little peaks, then Max held up the nipple clamps.

Yeah, they did kind of look like tweezers, but they had black rubber tips. He placed the first one on her nipple and, with his other hand, maneuvered the small metal ring up the tweezers until it tightened.

Sierra sucked in a breath as it tightened and tightened, then Max stopped. "Okay?"

"Green, Master."

It was as if Max was squeezing her nipple between his fingers. Moisture gathered in her pussy. Max then did the same to her right nipple. This time, she couldn't help but shift in her seat. Her pussy clenched the tighter the clamp got. Max tightened the left one to his satisfaction. The chain connecting the two clamps was draped right beneath her breasts.

"I won't leave them on too long." He turned. "Jordan, tell me when ten minutes have gone by." Max dipped his hand into his pocket and pulled out the bullet.

She jumped when he ran his hand over her stomach.

"Easy, sweet." He slid his finger down over the thong covering her pussy.

Her eyes shifted as she heard someone cough. Her body stiffened. Was she really going to allow him to do this?

"Focus on me, pet." His husky tone sent a jolt of awareness through her veins, and she turned her attention to him. His hazel eyes were on her face. "It's just us, baby. No one else exists."

"Yes, Master," she whispered.

His fingers stroked her over the thong until she let out a tiny moan. He grinned and slipped his fingers beneath the fabric.

"You're soaking wet, baby."

She couldn't deny it. Her pussy was clenching with need from his touch. What was it with him? She'd never reacted to a man like this. Her hips jerked when the cool bullet was pressed against her pussy.

It warmed quickly. Max shifted it until he had it in the position he wanted. Sierra let out a breath as he removed his fingers. While the toy felt unusual against her skin, she wondered why it seemed so special.

Max tugged the chain to the nipple clamps. A zing of pleasure shot from her nipples to her pussy, and she let out a moan.

That was unexpected.

He did it again as the bullet came to life.

Sierra jerked at the vibrations against her clit. They felt stronger than any vibrator she'd ever used. Her pussy clenched and heat filled her veins.

Max ran his fingers over her breasts, teasing them but he didn't tug on the chain again. "Your face is flushed," he whispered. "How are you doing?"

"Green, so far, Master."

His features were soft as he gazed at her, yet there was the heat of desire in his gaze. The bullet sped up, and he tugged the chain. That zing happened again, only stronger this time.

Her toes tingled, and her stomach clenched as her pussy contracted. *Holy crap!* "Don't fight it, baby," Max whispered, turning the bullet up again.

She shook her head. How could this be happening to her? She'd never climaxed easily, and within minutes, Max had her on the edge, just like he had that night at his house.

The vibrations increased, and Sierra cried out. Her toes curled as the tingling moved up her legs. "Master," she whispered, opening her eyes. When had she closed them?

"Let go, baby."

"I can't." She tugged at her wrists.

"Oh you can." He tugged the chain then put his hand against her groin. "Come for me, baby." He pressed his fingers against the bullet, putting more pressure on her clit.

"Fuck," she cried out as he moved the bullet side to side through the fabric. The tingling spread further, and she was trembling now. Need overwhelmed her.

Max shifted the bullet, and Sierra screamed as her climax hit. She thrashed in the restraints as he continued to manipulate the bullet. Sensations hit her one after the other.

"Time," Jordan yelled.

"Let go all the way, baby," Max said, then he jerked the chain so the clamps fell from her nipples.

Sierra closed her eyes as the blood rushing back into her nipples set off another explosion within her body. Her pussy clenched; her clit throbbed, and her nipples burned. She screamed again as she climaxed again.

"Fucking beautiful," Max whispered.

The bullet stopped vibrating, and Sierra slumped in the chair. Holy shit, she was never going to recover from this.

****

Max couldn't believe their first scene had gone so well. He released her arms, massaging them before moving to her legs. This woman responded to him on such a sensual level.

Jordan stood by with a warm blanket. "Go take care of her. I'll clean up for you."

"Thank you." Max draped the blanket over Sierra and picked her up. He carried her over to the sofas set aside for aftercare and sat down with her in his lap. Her eyes were closed, her head against his shoulder.

Her reactions to the bullet and the nipple clamps were so much more than he'd expected. He'd seen her nervousness at first with the crowd, but once he got her to focus on him, all her tension melted away.

Damon strode over and set a bottle of water on the side table with a grin, then walked away. His friends' support filled him with happiness. Yes, it had been a while since he'd taken on a sub, maybe because the last time he tried, it had ended in tragedy.

Max let out a sigh. Not that it had been much of a D/s relationship to begin with, but sometimes, being a man who wanted to fix everything, not being able to do that took a while to realize.

"You're frowning." Sierra's voice was as soft as her touch on his forehead. "Did I do something wrong, Master?"

"You were perfect." He bent his head and kissed her nose before he reached for the water. He twisted the cap off and put the bottle in her hand. "Drink."

192

Sierra held the bottle to her lips and took a swallow, then another and another until she'd consumed half the bottle before handing it back to him. "I didn't realize I was so thirsty."

"Our scene took a lot out of you. How do you feel?"

"Fine, Master." She glanced around the room, and her cheeks turned pink.

Max rubbed her cheek with his fingers. "Yes, they watched and heard you scream as you climaxed." Her cheeks grew darker, and Max curved his hand around the back of her neck. "You have nothing to be embarrassed about." He wanted her to know her reactions were fine and nothing to worry about. "Close your eyes, rest your head against my shoulder, and listen, sweetheart."

She did as he asked. He kept his hand on her neck, wanting to keep some skin-to-skin contact. A few minutes later, one of the other Doms approached. When Max nodded, he spoke. "Great scene, Master Max."

Another approached. "Responsive novice. You are very lucky, Master Max."

Then another Dom with his sub. "Enjoyed the scene, Master Max. If you have time in the next week, I'd like to get some pointers from you."

"Of course. Give me a call, and we'll set something up."

"Thank you."

Sierra shifted in his lap.

"See, my sweet."

"I don't understand. Don't all subs react like I did, Master?"

"No, they don't. Most novices are too inhibited the first few times they scene to climax, heck some of them freeze up or safeword out."

"But I assumed all subs climaxed with their Doms."

"It's a fine balance." He stroked her neck, enjoying the little shivers his touch caused. "Especially if a Dom is with a new sub. Trust takes time, and for some of the newer subs who don't have a regular Dom much more so."

"It's all very complicated."

"Like any relationship. That's why, in the kink community, communication is important. That's the reason we have the questionnaire, plus negations with the sub before we scene or play with them."

"I guess I just thought that was to make sure a sadist and a non-masochist weren't paired together."

Max let out a chuckle. "It's more than that. Most Doms and subs are attracted to each other on some level. It might just be sexually, but there usually has to be chemistry. I say some, not all, because you can't force something that isn't there."

"We have chemistry."

"Yes, we do." Big time, but he wasn't going to frighten her with that. "Some Doms and subs just play to release tension. But with a novice, as was mentioned, it usually takes a while to get comfortable enough to fully let go."

"What does it mean that I was able to?"

"That I'm a lucky bastard." He made no effort to suppress what he knew was a self-satisfied grin.

"Max," she whispered.

"I am." He took her lips in a quick hard kiss. "Your response was great. Once I got you to focus on me, you let all the tension drain from your body. How did you feel in the scene?"

"I liked it. And you're right. Once I forgot about the people watching us, I was able to concentrate on what you were doing to me."

"Did you enjoy what I did?"

Her lashes fell, blocking his view of her eyes, but not before he saw the flash of desire in them. "I did. Does that make me a bad person?"

"Hey." He slid his hand from the back of her neck, and cupped her cheek. "Baby, of course it doesn't. You received pleasure from what I did, and I got pleasure, as well."

"How did you get pleasure?" She squirmed on his lap. "I can feel your hard cock."

He couldn't dispute that. His dick had been hard from the moment she let him restrain her to the chair. "From watching you let go. Watching how your body flushed, how your breathing changed, the way your body reacted to *my* touch. There is nothing more beautiful than watching a woman orgasm because you caused her to."

"Can I do something for you?"

Max tilted his head and stared down at her. "What do you mean?"

"Will you allow me to give you pleasure?"

"Of course," he said the words automatically, not realizing Sierra meant now. She slipped from his lap, folded the blanket, dropped it at his feet, then knelt down. "Sierra," he started.

"Please, Master, let me do this."

Her blue eyes pleaded with him. "All right." It wasn't like him to concede, but he found he didn't want to refuse her.

Her smile lit up the room. She parted his legs, and slipped between them, then lowered the zipper on his pants. His cock sprang free.

She took a deep breath, and her fingers encircled his base. "Impressive, Master," she whispered, her breath brushing over his sensitive skin. Before he could respond, she leaned over and licked the head of his dick.

"Damn." His hips rose, and his hands gripped her shoulders.

"I should warn you, I haven't given a blow job very often. So forgive me if I don't get this completely right, Master."

He felt his glutes tense with the sensation of her moist, hot mouth on his cock. Her fingers on the base of his cock moved in time as she slid her mouth up and down. Every so often her tongue would trace one of the pulsing veins.

Max fought to keep his hands on her shoulders. Sierra was giving him a gift he'd never expected this soon. He wouldn't mess it up by trying to direct her. Not that she needed much direction.

With each pass of her mouth and hand, his cock grew harder. When her fingers brushed his balls, they drew up tight. Hell, he was primed and ready to explode. "Baby, I'm going to come. Lift your head and finish me off with your hand."

She barely pulled her mouth off his cock and said, "Not a chance."

Max's cock stiffened further at her words. She might not have done a blowjob in a while but her mouth was doing amazing things to him. When her fingers played with his balls this time, he didn't even try to hold back.

She sealed her lips around him as he spurted in her mouth. Her throat contracted with each pulse. Max collapsed against the sofa, and she licked the head of his cock like it was ice cream, then sat back and looked up at him.

Her blue eyes were shining, and her lips formed a satisfied little smile. Max leaned forward, grasped her by the arm and hauled her up onto his lap, and covered her lips with his.

He tasted his own salty mix, but didn't care. This woman had just given him a gift he hadn't asked for. When the kiss ended, clapping started. Sierra buried her face against his chest as he laughed.

"Fucking lucky Dom," someone said.

"Shit, did you see her? I've never seen a woman suck cock like that," another said.

"He didn't even ask; she just did it," yet another voice added.

Max waved them away as he stroked Sierra's back, enjoying the texture of her smooth skin against his palm. "You continually amaze me." He nuzzled her neck as he pushed his cock back into his pants and did up his zipper.

"I'm glad I can." Her breath brushed his chest.

"How about we take this to a more private place?" His dick was ready to go again.

Sierra looked up at him. "I'd love that."

Max's heart expanded as he waved Damon over. "I'm going to leave the club in yours and Jordan's hands. Don't disturb me unless the place is on fire."

"You got it." Damon replied, handing Max a fresh blanket.

Max pushed Sierra away from his chest and wrapped the blanket around her, then he stood with her in his arms and strode out of the club and out the back door. He took the path to his house.

"My things."

"We can get them later. They're safe."

"I can walk," she said, even though she snuggled close to him.

"Humor me." He loved having her in his arms.

He disarmed the alarm and punched in the code to open the patio door. Once inside, he reset the alarm and carried her to his bedroom. He lowered her to her feet next to his bed. "You are mine."

"Yes, I am, Sir."

Her soft words made his heart swell. He never thought he could fall for someone so fast, but with Sierra, it seemed natural. He pulled the blanket from her. "Lay in the middle of the bed."

She did as he asked. Max's cock swelled further. He couldn't wait to sink himself into her hot, moist depths. Going to the end of the bed, he stared at Sierra. Her blue eyes were on him. Good. Max stripped his clothing off, and then climbed onto the mattress.

He pushed her legs apart as he moved up the bed. Her skin flushed, and her breathing increased. Oh yes, his girl was aroused.

"You were so fucking beautiful tonight," he said between the kisses he peppered up her legs.

"You make me feel that way." Her voice was soft, and her fingers curled into the sheets.

"In my bedroom, you may touch me unless I direct you otherwise. I want your hands on me."

Her lips turned up when her fingers dug into his shoulders.

"You make me so hot."

"Well, prepare to get very hot." He hooked his fingers under the thong and pulled it off, tossing it to the floor. Now she was naked in front of him. He used his shoulders to keep her legs apart. "So pink, and wet." He drew his finger over her pussy.

"For you. Only you."

Max didn't say anything. He leaned down and swiped his tongue over her.

****

Sierra's hips lifted as Max's tongue licking over her entrance set her body on fire. What was it about him that made her so hot and wet? This wasn't the time to think about that.

Their play in the club, both on stage and later, when she sucked him off, still made her shiver with pleasure. She'd never been one who liked having a man's cock in her mouth, but with Max, it was heaven.

Maybe it was because he hadn't tried to force her. He'd kept his hands on her shoulders and didn't thrust into her mouth.

Her core tightened as he parted her labia and his tongue swept up to her clit, teasing it. Her nipples hardened and her clit tingled. It was sensitive after the bullet, but she relished the feel of his tongue playing with her. However, she wanted more. She wanted him.

"Max, please." She tugged at his shoulders.

"I will please you, baby." He moved over her. He reached over, pulled a condom from the bedside table and slipped it on.

His lips captured hers. She could taste her musky scent on his tongue. Part of her thought she should be repulsed by it, but another enjoyed it. Max had tasted himself when he kissed her at the club; it was only fair.

Their tongues dueled and tangled with each other as they shifted on the mattress. His cock rubbed against her pussy and Sierra moaned into the kiss. Max lifted his head.

"More," she whispered.

He grinned at her and shifted his hips. The tip of his hard dick brushed her entrance, then he thrust.

Sierra arched her neck as he penetrated her pussy. Oh Lord, he was hot and big. Her muscles stretched as he pushed forward, and his hot breath against her cheek made her pussy clench.

"Damn, baby. You're tight."

"And you're big."

"The words every man wants to hear."

She gave a little laugh and pulled her legs up, giving him more room.

"Such a hot, wet pussy." He pulled back and thrust in. Then did it again.

Sierra sensed the care he took. His arms shook with the strength it took to bide his time.

"Please, Max. Take me. I want you so much."

"I won't hurt you." His breathing was faster now.

"You won't." She curled her legs around his waist. "Fuck me, Max. Make me truly yours."

He let out a groan, and his lips took hers in a hard kiss, as he pulled back and slammed into her.

"Yes," she shouted into his kiss. Her pussy tightened around him and her clit throbbed. She wanted more.

Max gave it to her. In and out, until she had to break their kiss to breathe. Her nerves were alive and doing their own dance. Her toes curled as the pressure built inside her.

"Come now," Max growled in her ear.

Her body obeyed. Her pussy tightened and her climax rushed over her. But Max didn't stop thrusting. He kept moving, taking her higher and higher.

"Oh God, Max." She couldn't control her body anymore. Her hips met his, thrust for thrust, and her nails raked up and down his back.

"That's it, baby. Let it all go. Let me have it all." His voice was rough with need.

"I..." She cried out as another orgasm hit.

"More," he whispered as his fingers found her clit.

She shook her head, but his fingers were magic. They knew exactly how much pressure to put on her clit.

"Fuck," she screamed as another orgasm hit, her muscles tightening, and her pussy clenched down on his cock.

"Fuck yeah." Max thrust into her hard, then he came.

His face was expressive. Max's hot breath caressed her face, the little moans of pleasure as her pussy pulsed in time with his release. She panted, trying to find enough air to speak, but it just wasn't possible.

Max kissed her cheeks and forehead before placing a soft kiss on her lips. "Be right back." He lifted himself off her and his cock slipped from her pussy.

Her body trembled with the aftermath of their lovemaking. She turned her head to watch his sexy body as he walked into the bathroom. He wasn't gone long, and he returned with a grin on his face.

"My beautiful Sierra." He knelt on the bed and brushed his fingers over her cheek. "That was wonderful."

"I think that's my line, except I'd say it was fucking fantastic." She let out a yawn.

Max laughed. "Come on." He pulled her into his arms, then arranged the covers over them. "Sleep. We have all day tomorrow to be together."

"Yes." Tomorrow was Sunday, and she didn't have anything planned. Her lashes lowered. She snuggled up to Max.

****

Max stared down at Sierra as she slept. This was going beyond a Dom/sub club relationship, and he didn't mind. He'd known from the minute he met Sierra she was different. Now his heart agreed. He hoped she was feeling the same, because he didn't want to let her go. Ever.

Chapter Thirteen

On a Wednesday night, Sierra yawned as she, Tessa, and Crystal walked into the adult store. Tessa had convinced them to come with her to the new book club the store was starting up.

Thanksgiving had come and gone. She'd spent the day with Max cuddling on his sofa watching football and eating. She'd never had such a relaxing time with a man.

"Someone is burning the candle at both ends," Crystal teased.

"Yep," Sierra retorted. She and Max had spent every night together, and sometimes, that meant she didn't get a lot of sleep. "What is this book club about?" she asked Tessa.

"It's new. Destiny thought it would be a good idea, and since it's an adult store, it will be interesting to see what our first book will be."

"Go ahead and go in back," Destiny said from behind the counter. "I need to lock the door."

"You're closing while we're here?" That hadn't happened during Tessa's talk.

"Just this once. I don't have anyone to cover the counter."

The three women walked to the back and into the bookstore area. The front row was filled already. She turned to the second row. Sierra stopped in her tracks when she saw Max, Jordan, and Damon sitting there.

"Oh my," Crystal whispered.

"What?" Tessa asked, then saw the men. "Holy shit! Who ordered the hunks?" Her voice was barely above a whisper.

The men stood. Sierra shook her head. All three were dressed in black pants and shoes, but each had on a different color shirt. Max forest green, Jordan dark blue, and Damon deep burgundy.

Take a breath. Yes, the three men looked damn sexy, but only one stood out for her. Sierra smiled. "Hello, Max, Jordan, Damon." She nodded at each man as she said his name.

"Sierra." Max's deep voice sent shivers of excitement through her body. He took her hand in his, and a tremor raced through her. Damn, this man affected her. "I know Crystal." He looked over her shoulder.

"Crystal, you've met Max. The other two are Jordan, and Damon. Tessa, Max, Jordan, and Damon. Guys, these two are my best friends."

"Ladies." Max inclined his head.

"Please come sit down." Damon gestured to the chairs.

The women looked at each other, then moved, albeit slowly and in a bit of a fog. Somehow Tessa and Crystal ended up seated between Damon and Jordan, while Max made sure she was between him and Jordan.

"Sneaky," she whispered.

"Behave. The book club is about to begin," he said as Destiny walked in.

"Welcome everyone to Klineman's first book club night. I don't expect tonight to be long. We'll meet once a month, on Wednesday night." Her gaze took in the room. "So tonight, we have three books we can select from. How about I explain each one to the group?"

Forty-five minutes later, they stood. "This is going to be fun," Tessa said.

"Says the librarian." Crystal let out a laugh.

"So, you're a librarian?" Damon said to Tessa.

Tessa batted her eyelashes. "Yes, I am."

"Maybe you could help me. I'm looking for some older industrial engineering books."

"Oh Lord, don't get her started," Crystal complained.

"Behave," Sierra told her.

"And what do you do, Crystal?" Jordan asked.

"I'm a paralegal."

"You're *that* Crystal Hayden? The one who gave Judge Michaelson his nickname?" Jordan asked.

Crystal eyed Jordan with interest. "Are you an attorney?"

"Yep." Jordan answered.

"I knew you had a reputation," Tessa told Crystal.

Sierra couldn't help it; she burst out laughing at the wave of embarrassment on Crystal's face. Soon everyone was chuckling.

"So ladies, what do you say we all go out for coffee?" Max asked.

"Yes, let's." Sierra took Max's hand in hers.

* * * *

Crystal finished telling her story as they sat in the coffee shop. "And that's how Judge Michaelson got the nickname 'prune face'."

Jordan couldn't stop laughing. "I've always wondered. No one would talk about it."

Sierra looked at her friends and smiled. "How are you doing?" Max asked softly in her ear. "We haven't talked much lately."

205

"And whose fault is that?" She smiled. "Not that I've minded."

"For all the screaming, I thought not."

Heat filled her face. Max had a way of throwing her off balance. "Work is busy, but otherwise everything is fine." And it really was. Sometimes it scared her how happy she was.

Her friends were having fun tonight. She was impressed with the way Jordan and Damon pulled the two women out of their shells, not that Crystal and Tessa were shy. Well, Tessa did have a tendency to be a little quiet. Just then raised voices caught their attention.

A couple with a little boy across the coffee bar were arguing. The little boy looked uncomfortable.

"Oh no," Crystal whispered.

Sierra's stomach cramped. The look on the little boy's face hit close to home with her. She grasped Max's arm. "Should we do something?"

Max kept his gaze on the couple. "They're only arguing."

"But look at the boy's face," Tessa said. "He's scared." Tessa's fingers closed around her coffee cup, gripping it hard.

"Most are when their parents argue," Damon said, putting his arm around her shoulders.

"Max?" Sierra started to stand.

"I can't stand it," Crystal stood first. "I have to intervene."

"Crystal," Jordan said as he stood. "That may not be a good idea." His tone was soft, but Sierra heard the command behind it.

"No, this isn't right." Crystal stared up at him. "I will not allow this." She marched across the room with Jordan close behind her.

Sierra let out a sigh. "One of Crystal's last cases involved child abuse."

"She was really torn up about that case," Tessa said.

"No one should hurt a child," Damon muttered.

"No, children are precious." The group watched as Crystal and Jordan approached the table. The couple looked up. Jordan stepped in front of Crystal and Sierra watched her friend stiffen.

Oh no, that wasn't good. Jordan was speaking for Crystal. Her friend wasn't going to take that lightly.

The couple's mouths dropped open, and Sierra realized Jordan had said something. They shook their heads, and then the mother scooped her son up into her arms and hugged him close.

The man stood and shook Jordan's hand, then Jordan took Crystal's arm and led her back to the table.

"I could have handled it," Crystal said pulling her arm away from Jordan as she sat down.

"It was just an argument. They didn't even realize what was happening with their son." Jordan stared at her. "You were about to go off on them. They didn't deserve that.

"And you didn't?" Crystal crossed her arms over her chest. "You weren't exactly mincing your words." Sierra sat back and watched her friend. It wasn't like Crystal to be so confrontational.

"No, I didn't. But I said it in a calm voice, and you saw how they reacted. They were horrified they were scaring their son." Jordan took a breath and put his hand over Crystal's.

"Did you see the mother's face?"

Crystal withdrew her hand from Jordan's. "I did." A sigh left her lips. "I'm sorry." Tears filled her eyes.

Max slipped his arm around Sierra's shoulders.

"Excuse me." Crystal ran outside.

Sierra started to get up, but Max tightened his arm around her. She opened her mouth, and Max shook his head.

"Let me go take care of Crystal," Jordan said, as he stood and followed.

"Take care of Crystal?" Tessa's voice held a note of surprise. "Sierra, we should go to Crystal."

"Let Jordan handle it," Damon said.

"Jordan doesn't know her; we do." Tessa shot back.

"Sassy woman," Damon tapped her nose with his finger.

Tessa lifted her chin, and her brown eyes grew cold and hard.

"Oh crap," Sierra whispered.

"What?" Max asked.

"Tessa doesn't take well to men telling her what to do."

"Do not tell me what to do." Tessa glared at Damon. "You are an ass, Damon." Tessa stood, then gave Sierra a pointed look. "I'm ready to go home."

"I'll take you," Damon said.

"Like hell you will. I'm done with you." Tessa gave him her hard librarian stare. "I'll meet you at the car, Sierra." Tessa stomped out of the cafe. Damon shook his head and followed her.

Max burst out laughing. "Your friends are something else."

"They are. I love them, but we better go after them before one of them starts World War Three." She stood. Her friends had strong opinions, and coming up against two Doms could have made the rest of the evening very interesting—for the Doms.

Max took her hand as they left the cafe. By the time they arrived at Tessa's car, Tessa and Crystal were inside, with Jordan and Damon standing next to the vehicle.

"Thanks for the coffee," Sierra said to Max.

"You're welcome." He cupped her cheeks and gave her a kiss. "See you this weekend."

"Yep." Sierra opened the passenger door and climbed in. Tessa started the car and roared out of the parking lot.

****

Max turned to the two men. "I think you two didn't make any friends tonight."

"Are you kidding?" Damon said. "That woman got my engines going."

"Crystal is a fire cracker as well. It should be fun to see what happens the next time we see them."

"Mmmhmm. And if you're lucky, you both might get away with your testicles intact." Max shook his head at his friends, but he was happy they were interested in the women.

* * * *

"Would either of you two like to tell me what happened last night?" Sierra looked at her two friends over lunch at Lara's café the next day.

Tessa's face turned red, and Crystal sighed.

"I'm sorry. My last case got to me, and when I saw that couple fighting and the little boy's face, I lost it," Crystal said.

"I get it," Sierra reached over and patted her friend's hand. "We all have our hot buttons, but that doesn't explain your rudeness, Tessa."

Crystal looked at Sierra and then Tessa. "Rude? Tessa is never rude."

"I was last night." Tessa shook her head. "I don't know what came over me. When Damon told me to let Jordan handle you, I told him he was an ass."

"So that's why you stormed out of the café with him hot on your heels." Crystal rested her elbow on the table and settled her chin in the palm of her hand.

"I didn't think you noticed. You were hanging all over Jordan." Tessa said.

"She was? How'd I miss that?"

"Max kept you busy," Tessa said with a smile. "So is it serious?"

Her friends looked at her. "Changing the subject are we?" Sierra raised her eyebrows, but her friends kept their gazes on her. "We've only known each other a few weeks."

"Yet you're playing with him at the club," Tessa said.

"And you didn't come home again last Saturday night," Crystal added.

"How the hell do you know that?" Sierra stared at her friend.

"Gotcha." Crystal clapped her hands. "I knew it. You slept with him."

"Keep your voice down." Sierra glanced around the café. It wasn't crowded yet, but soon would be. "Yes, I slept with Max."

"Oh my goodness," Tessa whispered. "How was it?" She slapped her hand over her mouth. "I can't believe I asked that."

"Heck, I want to know if they had regular sex or kinky," Crystal said, her eyes twinkling.

"Sex is sex," Sierra said. "We had a scene Saturday night, and both of us needed more than that. Max took me to his house, and I spent the night with him." And all day Sunday. Max had shown her how fun it was to go skinny-dipping in a private, heated pool.

"You have to get us passes to this club," Crystal said.

"What?" Sierra couldn't have heard her friend right.

"She's right. I'd love to see what the club is like," Tessa said.

Sierra sat back in her chair. "You two are serious." Their eyes sparkled with excitement and something else, interest. In the club or in the two men they met last night? This could be interesting.

"Yep." Crystal crossed her arms over her chest. "I'm curious after all the books I've read."

Tessa just nodded.

"I'll talk to Max and see what he says. I'm still a provisional member myself. You might need to go through the orientation classes." Her friends were interested in Wicked Sanctuary. Her mind grappled with the information. Although she thought it was great, it was unexpected.

"That's fine," Crystal said.

"Have you picked up more work?" Sierra asked Crystal. Her friend was a good paralegal, but she only took the jobs she wanted instead of working for one or two lawyers full-time.

"Not yet. There's talk about a big civil case coming up. There's very little information on it, but if it's as big as some are saying, I'm sure the lawyers will be looking for some help."

Sierra nodded. "That will make you a tidy sum."

"Yep." Crystal turned her head. "Tessa, how are things at the library?"

"Fine. They're finally allowing me some more buying power, so I need to pour over catalogs and check where I can purchase books. I'm going to expand our romance section."

"Does that mean a promotion?" Sierra asked. The Pleasant Valley library wasn't a big one. It was part of the bigger county system, but the county was allowing the libraries to run themselves without too much interference.

"Not yet. I don't mind." Tessa's eyes widened, and Sierra looked behind her. A group of bikers had walked in.

Big guys in leather and tats. They strode over to one of the tables and sat down. A couple at a nearby table got up and left. Sierra looked at the counter. Lara stood there shaking her head.

One of the bikers stood and walked up to the counter. Sierra kept her gaze on Lara. Lara smiled, nodded, wrote down what he said, then took his money and gave him his change. When Lara turned to prepare his order, the man stuffed a twenty into the tip jar, and walked back to the table.

"I'm not sure having the bikers here is helping Lara's business," Tessa said.

"Why not?" It looked like they ordered and tipped well.

"Did you see the look the couple gave the bikers before they walked out?" Tessa asked.

"They're not hurting anyone." Sierra wrinkled her nose. Why couldn't people see the good in people rather than the bad?

"They're delicious," Crystal said.

"Oh brother, there goes bad girl Crystal," Sierra said with a laugh.

"Stop it." Crystal laughed, and the men looked in their direction.

"Where did they come from? I don't remember there being a lot of bikers here?" Sierra asked. Pleasant Valley was a small town.

"There's a new shop opening down the street. It's a leather shop that caters to the bikers," Tessa said.

"Damn. You know everything," Crystal said.

Tessa smiled. "It comes from working in a public library, you hear everything when people come in." Tessa pointed a finger at Sierra. "So when are you seeing Max again?"

"Tomorrow night," Sierra said.

"Good, oh damn." Tessa looked at her watch. "I need to get to work." She stood up. "Sunday. Brunch at your apartment. And I want to know details."

Sierra shook her head. "I guess I'm on the hook for brunch."

"I'll bring stuff. So will Tessa. What do you say, Sierra? Want to go get a pedicure? I could use a little pampering."

"Let's do it." Sierra had a mountain of work, but she wanted to do something special for Max tomorrow night. The women stood.

Lara took food over to the bikers. After she set it all down, they thanked her and began to eat.

Nice, polite guys, Sierra thought.

* * * *

Max looked at Sierra's toes and burst out laughing. "Kittens?" His hazel eyes twinkled.

"It seemed appropriate, Sir." He'd called her kitten a few times. Sierra looked around the club. It was a night where a member could bring guest. That answered her question about bringing Crystal and Tessa. She'd have to talk to Max about it later.

"Very much so." He lowered his voice. "You're my kitten, no one else's."

Sierra grinned at him. She loved being his. "Of course, Sir."

"I'm on duty, so if you want, find a scene you want to observe, and I'll have one of the other Doms watch over you while I take care of business."

Sierra looked around the room. She really did want to learn more about flogging. "I'd like to go to the flogging station."

Max's eyebrows rose, but he didn't say anything. He cupped her elbow and led her over to the sofa. Sierra sat down, now not as self-conscious of how undressed she was. She was enjoying the way the deep blue corset accented her breasts. While the short skirt showed her ass, at least she had a thong on. Max was very understanding about how she wasn't ready for full nudity yet.

"Let me see," Max said as he looked around the club. "Ah, Colby. Can I borrow you for a bit?"

"Sure, Max, what do you need?"

Sierra looked at Colby. Tall like Max, but Colby had short dark hair and a slightly crooked nose, and he wore leather pants and a black tank.

"Colby, this is my sub, Sierra. Would you mind staying with her while I take care of my duties for a bit?"

"Not at all, Max. Permission to sit with her and talk to her?"

"Of course." Max leaned down. "Colby will take good care of you. You have my permission to interact with him." Max captured her lips in a hard kiss before striding away.

Colby sat down next to her. "It's very nice to meet you, sub Sierra."

"You too, Sir."

"Please, call me Colby." He grinned.

"If you'll call me Sierra."

"Deal." He looked toward the scene that was being set up. "So you're interested in flogging?"

"Yes and no. I'm trying to comprehend the difference between flogging and a beating." She wrinkled her nose. "I don't quite understand why anyone would allow someone to hurt them."

"Ah, but that's the key. It's not about pain, it's about pleasure."

"Can you explain that to me?" She really wanted to understand.

"Maybe Max should do that?"

Sierra shook her head. "Max is busy, and I'd like your opinion."

"All right. Let's start with how much you know about flogging."

****

Two hours later, Max looked over at Sierra and Colby, both watching another flogging scene. Colby leaned over and said something, and Sierra nodded. Good. He'd hoped she'd be comfortable enough to ask Colby questions.

He was aware Sierra was curious about some of the play in the club, but she wasn't comfortable asking him about it. He wasn't sure if that was because she was embarrassed, or she was afraid he'd push her limits. He'd have to make it clear he wouldn't do that, and there was no reason to be shy. He wanted her to ask questions.

"We might have a situation," Jordan said, walking up to him.

"What?"

"Sage just came in, and Brady is with her."

"Damn, I thought they're not supposed to be seeing each other." Max ran a hand over the back of his neck. He liked Sage and Brady, but they were both involved in a court case.

"Yeah. I can't talk to them together since I'm Sage's lawyer."

"I'll go talk to them." Max strode across the room to the Domme and her sub.

"Evening, Max," Sage said when he approached.

"Sage." Max looked over at Brady. "You two cannot play."

Sage let out a sigh. "I know. Brady just came over to say hi." She looked at her sub with sad eyes. "Go, my pet. We can't take any chances."

"Yes, Ma'am." Brady left, his shoulders slumped.

"I feel bad about this, Sage." Max hated having to separate the pair. How would he feel if he was forced to leave Sierra alone? Not happy.

"Don't." Sage took a deep breath. "I just had to see him to make sure he was okay." She lifted her chin. "Is Jordan around, I have a couple questions for him, and then I'll leave."

"You don't have to leave." Max wanted to be sure she understood she was still welcome in the club, as was Brady.

"Thank you, but it's better that I do, otherwise I'll want to play with Brady."

"All right. Stay here and I'll send Jordan over." Max opened his arms, and Sage stepped into them. He hugged her tight. "It will be over soon."

"God, I hope so."

Max released her and motioned to Jordan and sent him to Sage's side. The flogging scene had ended and so had his shift. He walked over to Colby and Sierra. Sierra was frowning at him.

Colby stood. "It was a pleasure to talk with you, Sierra." Colby turned to Max. "She's a keeper." They shook hands, and Colby leaned close as he walked by. "She saw the hug you gave Sage. You might explain."

"Thank you." So that's what her frown was about. "My duties are done." He said holding his hand out to her.

Sierra put her hand in his, but Max felt the small tremor that shook her body. He pulled her to her feet and into his arms. "The woman I hugged was Sage. She's one of the Dommes here. She's going through a rough time right now and needed a hug."

To her credit Sierra ducked her head and her cheeks turned pink. "Sorry, Sir."

Max put his fingers under her chin and tilted her head. "Communication. I'd rather have you yell at me than to go off upset over something that is easily explained."

"I think I can handle that."

"She's mine," a raised male voice said.

"No, she's mine," another said.

"Be right back," Max said, annoyed that he had to leave Sierra to break up this argument before it turned into a fight.

Sierra watched Max until a man she hadn't seen before stepped in front of her. "Let's play," he said grabbing her hand.

She frowned. First, that wasn't how one should negotiate, and second, touching without permission was a no-no. She yanked her hand from his and held up her arm showing her purple and white wristband. "I'm taken."

He shook his head and gave her a creepy grin. "Who cares? I want to scene with you." This time he took her by the upper arm and pulled her toward the flogging scene.

Sierra glanced around for help, but all the attention was on the guys yelling. Damn. She was getting tired of men dragging her off whenever they thought they could.

"Red," she screamed out.

The room went silent. Damon reached her side first. "Sierra?" He looked from her to the guy holding her arm.

"This person isn't paying attention." She refused to call the idiot a Dom. A Dom wouldn't act like he did. "I showed him and told him I was taken." She held up her banded arm. Her heart pounded, and her nerves danced. Max told her the rules, and if someone broke them it was on them, not her.

Damon turned to the man when Max walked up.

"Let her go. Now."

Max's tone caused a shiver to run over Sierra's skin. It was that low 'I am pissed' tone. She bit back a smile when the man dropped her arm like a hot potato.

Max drew her to his side, tilting her chin up. "Are you okay, my kitten?"

"I'm fine now." She snuggled to his side. She always felt safe with Max. Sierra's insides froze. She truly felt safe with Max; there was no doubt about it. That was new for her, and it was going to take time to sort through her feelings.

"I don't recognize you," Max said to the man.

"I'm sorry, Master Max," one of the other Doms said, walking up to them. "Ray is my guest for the evening." He looked at his friend. "I told you the rules, Ray. One of them is no touching."

"I wanted to play, not listen to lectures," Ray whined.

"I didn't realize Ray had snuck out while Master Jordan went over the rules," the Dom said.

"He obviously needs them. Harry, he's violated the rules of consent. He needs to go."

"I understand, Master Max." Harry took his friend's arm and pulled him away. "Damn it, Ray, I told you about consent. Now you've blown your only chance."

"Damn, I've never heard you that calm under similar circumstances. What's going on?" Damon asked.

"Maybe I'm mellowing out," Max said.

Sierra laughed and muttered, "Yeah right." Her ass was still tender from last night and him showing her how sensual swats on the ass could be. "Behave." He leaned down. "Or I will spank you here in front of everyone."

219

"Yes, Master." She turned her head to look at Damon. "Thank you for your help, Master Damon."

"My pleasure. I'm glad you yelled the safe word." He grinned and left.

"I did the right thing, didn't I?" Sierra glanced up at Max.

"You did." He pulled her flush to his body. "That is always what you should do if you are ever in a situation in which you did not consent or want whatever is happening to come to an immediate halt. Just like you did that night in the reception area. Our attention was elsewhere." He frowned for a moment, then, staring down at her, his frown disappeared. "What do you think if we leave a little early and take this party to my house?"

"As my Sir wishes."

One look at his sub and everything else melted away. Max smiled and maneuvered Sierra around. He found having her in his home and bed more fun than the club. Not that they wouldn't have club play, but until she got more comfortable, they'd take it private.

They hadn't even taken two steps when a blond woman wearing next to nothing dropped to her knees in front of him. Max let out a sigh. "Sorry, I'm..." The words died on his lips when the blonde lifted her head. "Angelina?"

"I'm finally here, Max. And I'll give you my complete and total submission."

What the hell was his ex-wife doing here? She'd never been interested in kink when they were together.

"How did you get in?"

Ralph was meticulous; he wouldn't have just let her walk in.

"I came with a friend." Angelina shifted on her knees, moving closer to him. "I'm yours, Max."

He shook his head. "No, you are not."

"He's taken." Sierra's voice was tinged with anger. His arm tightened around her waist.

"He was mine first," Angelina said, glaring at Sierra.

Sierra took a step back. "This is your ex-wife?" Her voice held disbelief as she slid from his hold.

"Yes."

Max ran a hand over his face. This night was turning into one big clusterfuck.

Angelina shifted again, wrapping her arms around one of his legs. "Hands off," he barked. Angelina dropped her hand, but frowned at him. "Whose guest is this?" Max bellowed. First, the guys fighting over a sub, then the guy trying to scene with Sierra without consent, and now this.

No one spoke up. He wanted to know who'd brought this woman into his club. Hell, the club hadn't even been built when they divorced. She shouldn't even know about this place. Something wasn't right here.

"Who brought you, Angelina?" He glanced around the club. While everyone watched, no one came forward to claim that they'd brought Angelina. Regina moved up beside Sierra, Jordan and Damon to Max's left.

"She came in with...I don't know his name," Regina said, looking around. "I don't see him, Master Max."

"He doesn't matter, only you do," Angelina said again. "I'm yours and yours only." She rose to her feet, and before he could stop her, her lips locked on his.

****

221

Sierra stood stunned. This was Max's ex. The one he said wasn't into kink. Yet here she was, on her knees in front of him, wearing next to nothing and telling him she was his.

Insecurities welled up in Sierra. His ex was perfect. Perfect hair, perfect makeup, perfect body. All Sierra could hear was her father's voice telling her she'd never be that beautiful. She couldn't compete with that. Did she really want to? No, she'd always lose against someone like that.

Hell, his ex declared she wanted to be Max's submissive, totally submissive. Sierra would never again hand control of every aspect of her life to someone else, even someone she loved. Yes, she'd sit on her knees and lean on Max's legs, but that was in private, never in the club. While she enjoyed letting go in the club, she didn't think she could ever be as free as his ex was.

Sierra looked at Max. He seemed surprised to see his ex. While they'd spent last night together, Max had been a little secretive over the last few days. Her heart shuddered. Was this why?

Tears welled in her eyes.

Max didn't push his ex away as she kissed him. Sierra's mouth went dry. "I need to go," she whispered to Regina.

"Sierra—" Regina said.

Sierra didn't wait to hear what Regina had to say. She hadn't taken two steps, though, when Max reached for her. Sierra danced away from him.

Hurt reflected in his eyes.

"I'm sorry, Max." She fought to keep the tears from falling. "I can't be what you want." She turned and ran out of the room.

It took her three tries to get her locker open, she was shaking so hard. Not only because she was upset, but because she was afraid Max would follow her. Sierra yanked a t-shirt over her outfit, thinking about all the time they'd spent together. All the times they'd played, their conversations, holding hands. Twisting her wristband this way and that, she couldn't stop the replay in her mind.

Sierra yanked the band off her wrist and threw it in the locker. She'd been living in a dream world.

Regina came into the room and opened her own locker. "I'm driving you home." She quickly put on a pair of pants and a shirt.

"Regina..."

"Keys." She held her hand out. "You're in no shape to drive."

Sierra had to agree with her. She could barely see through the haze of tears. She fumbled for the keys in her purse and dropped them into Regina's palm. "Let's go."

Sierra followed Regina out. She could hear raised voices in the club, but she didn't care. Ralph stood by the door. He opened it and nodded to Regina.

"Thanks, Ralph. You're a good man," Sierra said.

Her heart broke with every step as she walked to her car. She wasn't sure how she was going to pick up the pieces this time. Because, in the club, she'd been right.

She loved Max.

Chapter Fourteen

Max took a deep breath and then knocked on Sierra's apartment door. Nothing. His heart sank.

"Sierra, honey." He placed his hand against the cold wood. "We can talk this out? Please just open the door."

What would happen if she didn't? He didn't want to think about it, but he had to accept that as a possibility. Max put his back against the jam of the door and slid down to the floor.

"I know it looked bad." He rested his head against the door to her apartment. "She means nothing to me, Sierra. I wish you would talk me." Max just kept talking, he didn't know what else to do. After an hour, he stood up and straightened his clothes.

"I'm going to go now. I'll call you and I hope you'll pick up. Please, Sierra don't give up on us."

His heart hurt with each step he took away from her. Maybe, just maybe, she'd been listening.

* * * *

"Fuck." Max slammed his cell-phone on the table.

"She still won't answer?" Jordan said.

"No. It's been two days. I can't get her to answer her phone. She won't answer her door, and she hasn't been to work. Her receptionist said she's on vacation." Max blew out a breath. This was such a royal fuck-up. He needed Sierra to talk to him.

"Maybe it's time to take drastic action," Damon said.

"Like what?" Max wasn't sleeping or eating. He'd kicked Angelina out, and Jordan had warned her that, if she talked about the club, her ass would end up in court before she could finish the first sentence.

"Go to her apartment and camp outside her door," Damon said.

"I don't even know if she's there."

"She is." Jordan leaned forward. "Crystal told me Sierra's been holed up there."

"Thanks, but it's too late tonight." It was almost midnight.

"Then go first thing in the morning. You need to talk to her," Damon said.

"I do." He rubbed his tired eyes.

"Go get some sleep. You want to be fresh and handsome when you see her tomorrow," Jordan said.

"That is if she'll even talk to me." Where were these negative thoughts coming from? Seeing Angelina again had messed with his head, and he'd gotten even more messed up when Sierra walked out. Max had never expected to see his ex-wife again, let alone kneeling at his feet. It was all a game to Angelina. She didn't like kink, and while they were married, she didn't care if he played at a club as long as he didn't have sex. He didn't have a problem with that, but then she freaked out when he took on a sub.

Sierra. His heart tightened. The fear he'd been suppressing that she was more intrigued about the lifestyle than having a committed relationship with him came roaring out when she walked out the door of the club. He was a Dom, for goodness sake; he shouldn't have these kinds of doubts, but he was human. Tomorrow. He'd go to her place and try again.

"Positive thinking," Damon said.

Max shook his head. He'd been so lost in his thoughts, it took him a minute to realize what Damon meant. "I'll try. Thanks, guys."

"Hey, what are friends for?" Jordan said.

* * * *

Sierra sighed as someone pounded on her door. She rubbed her nose. Maybe it was time to face Max and have this out. She'd avoided him for the past three days, but her mind was such a jumbled mess. With a sigh, she opened the door without looking through the peephole.

"About time, girl."

Sierra was stunned as her father pushed past her into her apartment, followed by...her ex-boyfriend?

"What are you doing here?" Her gaze went from Carl to her father and back again. "Carl, you're violating the restraining order." Damn, she should have known he wouldn't listen to the courts. "And I haven't seen you in over ten years," she said to her father.

"I've come to get you under control, you little slut."

Sierra winced at his language, but she was older now and more in control of her life. "Sorry, Dad." She glanced over her shoulder. "Nope. No sluts here. I want both of you to leave now."

Where had this inner strength come from? The answer hit her like a hurricane force wind.

Max.

Max showed her how strong she was. While she might be submissive to Max and want him to take control in the bedroom, she controlled her life. She was the one that determined who she gave up control to.

Thank you, Max, she said silently. Sadness hit her that she couldn't be the complete submissive Max wanted. Sierra reached for her cell phone.

"I don't think so," Carl said. Snatching her cell phone, he threw it against the wall, smashing it.

"Carl, do you really want to get thrown in jail again?" She had to be smart about this. It was Wednesday, so most of her neighbors were at work. Crystal might be home, but she'd mentioned something about a job. Sierra was on her own. Her stomach clenched.

She thought of everything she'd learned about herself since Max came into her life. He knew she had strength. He'd helped her see that in herself. Sierra straightened. She could do this.

"Carl told me about you doing all sorts of things with a man who is not your husband. Nasty things that are a sin against God."

What had Carl told her father? And how the hell did he know anything about her life since they broke up? It didn't matter. "It's my life. Now get the hell out of my apartment. I don't want either of you here." Her voice rose.

"When are you going to learn not to talk back to your father?".

Sierra's heart froze when her father took a step toward her.

* * * *

Max heard the raised voice the moment he hit the hallway to Sierra's apartment. He stood just beyond the entrance to her apartment, where he could hear but not see anything.

"You are nothing but a worthless slut," a man's voice yelled.

"And you're nothing but an abuser," Sierra yelled back. "This is my life; it has nothing to do with you. Get out of my house."

"You're just like your mother."

"I'll take that as a complement."

Who was the man she was arguing with?

"Sierra, listen to your father," another male voice said.

"Stay out of this, Carl. I don't know how you hooked up with my father, and I don't care. I want both of you out of here."

"This young man told me of your sinful ways."

"I don't care if you think they're sinful. It's my life. I'm not that scared teenager anymore. I will live my life the way I want, without any interference from you or Carl, who, by the way, will soon be arrested for violating a restraining order."

Fuck. Max backed down the hallway and took out his cell. "Hey, Logan, Max here. Sierra's ex-boyfriend is violating the restraining order you put in place for her. Can you get to her place now?"

"On my way with two units. We'll turn off the sirens as we approach so we don't tip him off."

"Thanks." Max put his phone away and moved back to the doorway, still out of sight. He wanted to jump in and make sure Sierra was safe, but he had to trust her. He'd only interfere if one of the two men tried to take Sierra out of her apartment or hurt her. She was a strong woman who could handle herself. He believed in her.

"She didn't understand," Carl whined when Max returned to his post.

Max cursed; he missed part of the conversation.

"There was nothing to understand." The frustration in Sierra's voice came through loud and clear.

That's his girl. Standing up to the two bullies. And that's what they were. Neither cared for Sierra the way he did.

"It doesn't matter," the older male voice said, which Max now knew was her father. "Maybe it's time I finally beat the sin out of you."

Max took a step forward, then stopped.

"Like hell," Sierra yelled. "You might be my biological father, but you come near me, and I'll make you wish you hadn't."

You go, Sierra.

"Carl, grab her."

Oh fuck no. Max took another step forward when a hand on his arm stopped him. "We'll take care of it." It was Logan, with five other police officers. Relief hit Max in the stomach. Let the law take care of it, but it was replaced with fear the second he heard a scream.

There were several thumps from inside Sierra's apartment after the scream. The officers raced past Max and rushed the door. Max followed, blinking when he saw the situation. Carl was curled up on the floor, his hands cupping his groin. The older man was backed up against the wall with Sierra's arm at his throat, her back to the door.

Sierra looked over her shoulder, and her eyes widened.

"Sierra, you can let him go. We'll take it from here," Logan said, keeping his tone calm and even.

"Sure." Sierra released the man. She stepped back and dusted off her hands like she'd touched something dirty.

Before anyone could move, the older man raised his hand and slapped Sierra. "You're no daughter of mine."

Max stepped forward, but Logan stopped him.

The man glared at Sierra and the police. "I'm leaving," he said.

"No, you're not." One of the officers stepped forward and grasped her father by the arm. "Ms. Blake, do you want to press charges for assault?"

Sierra was silent, her hand on her cheek. She shook her head. "No officer, but I would appreciate it if you'd get him out of here." She looked down at Carl on the floor. "Him, I'll press charges against for violating a restraining order."

"That we can do," the officer said.

Logan released Max's arm, and Max maneuvered around everyone to get to Sierra's side. "Baby, you okay?"

"You're here," she whispered.

"Where else would I be?" He pulled her into his arms. "You were magnificent."

"I hope you both burn in hell." The venomous words of her father caused Sierra to stiffen in Max's arms.

"Enough," the officer said, pushing her father out of her apartment, with one officer following. The other three officers picked Carl up and marched him into the hallway.

"I'll need a statement from you later, Sierra," Logan said, then he looked at Max. "Just call me when you're ready." Logan left the apartment, shutting the door behind him.

"I'm sorry my father said that to you."

Max gazed down at her. Her blue eyes held a hint of sadness.

"He's a bitter old man."

"Yeah, he is."

"You don't ever need to apologize for him." He rubbed his finger over her red cheek. "Do you need some ice?"

"I'm okay."

Max didn't know what to say, he wanted to keep her in his arms, but they needed to talk. "Can we sit down and talk?"

Sierra let out a sigh. "I don't know."

He sucked in a breath. Had he screwed this up that much? It didn't matter; he had to try. "You fought your dad and Carl for your independence. Are you not willing to fight for us?" He didn't want to believe she'd given up on him. Them.

"I want to..." Her words trailed off.

Max took the opening. He lifted her into his arms and carried her the sofa. He sat and put her in his lap. His dominant side wasn't going to wait another second. If she told him to get lost after he made his case, so be it.

"What is it with you holding me in your lap?"

"This way you can't escape." He ran a finger over her lips. "Talk to me."

"And say what?" She closed her eyes.

"Something? Anything?" Was this it? Was she going to give up everything they had together?

"It won't work, Max."

"What?"

"Us."

"Why not?" Okay, she was talking. Not saying what he wanted to hear, but talking.

"I can't be what you want."

The anguish in her voice and face tugged at his heart. "What is it you think I want?" What expectations did she have built up in her mind? How much damage did Carl and her father do before he got here?

"I'm not like your ex-wife."

"Thank God for that. She's a damn bitch." Her eyes went wide, and the knot in Max's stomach started to loosen. "She only came to the club to make trouble." He lowered his head. "I haven't seen Angelina since the divorce, where she cleaned out most of my bank account."

"She what?"

"Money is all Angelina cares about. She didn't know about the trust fund my parents set up." He hated talking about this part of his past, but if they were going to get through this, he needed to be open and honest. "When Angelina and I first met, I'd just made my first million in IT, then the video games took off. I was foolish and we married. She really didn't want a marriage or anything that tied her down."

"You said she didn't like kink," Sierra's voice was soft, but at least she wasn't trying to escape his embrace.

"She didn't and doesn't. We grew apart because of it, and a part of myself was missing. With her permission, I'd go out with Damon and Jordan, but it wasn't enough. I needed more."

"The kink part wasn't enough?"

"Yes and no." How did he explain this to her? Honestly. "Sex with Angelina was okay, but I wanted more. At the clubs or parties, there was never a connection between me and my sub. It didn't take long to realize I wanted that connection." He took a deep breath. "The connection we have."

Sierra's eyes widened as she looked up at him. "You didn't want your ex-wife the other night?"

"I'm guessing you didn't hear my confession at your apartment the other day."

"Confession? Was that on Sunday?"

"Yes."

"I was at Crystal's place. I needed some time."

"I get that. But honestly, why the hell would I want my ex when I have the woman of my dreams?" Max leaned down and rested his forehead against hers as his arms tightened around her. "Sierra, it's you I want, not some fake, blonde woman who wants to play games."

"But she said she'd be your complete submissive. And you didn't tell her no. You wanted that. I saw it in your face. I can't be that. I don't have that in me."

"I don't want a complete submissive. How can I fix this?" Max shook his head.

"Max." She placed her palm on his cheek. "You take on too much responsibility. You don't have to fix everything." He opened his mouth, and she placed her fingers over his lips. "I know you want to, but sometimes you have to let others shoulder the responsibility."

"That's another thing I love about you. You have an inner strength that most women don't have. You call me out and can be submissive, but only with a man you trust." He lifted his head and framed her face with his palms. "I love the way you submit to me in the bedroom, and in the club. I love that you trust me. Only me. That's what I need, what I crave."

"Are you saying you don't want my submission in other aspects of your life?" Her tone held astonishment.

"There might be times where I want your submission outside the bedroom. Like when we're home alone and I want to see my lover naked in the family room, or bent over the island in the kitchen taking my cock into her sweet pussy." Color flooded her cheeks. "If I ask you for something that crosses a line, then tell me. We will talk about it. I respect you." He leaned down and brushed his lips over hers. "I love you, Sierra."

"You do?" she whispered.

"I do. I've watched you with your friends, your concern for them, but also caring for them. You have girls' night. You're passionate about your work. I saw or should I say heard that when you took a call on a Sunday to make sure the grants you approve are going to the right place. And lastly, at the club. You sit in the green area talking with the other subs when I'm busy. Many of them have come up to me to tell me how much they enjoy talking with you. I love your body, your mind. I love you."

"Oh Max." Her eyes went glassy.

"I mean it, Sierra. I'm thankful for the day you walked up to my club, soaking wet, and thawed my heart, my soul. I'd hidden myself from the world because of my ex. You've shown me the man I could become."

Tears spilled down her cheeks. "Max, I was hurt, thinking you wanted your ex and not me."

"Never in a thousand years." He crushed her to him.

"I'm sorry I walked out. I was so confused." Her arms encircled his neck. "My father always told me I was worthless, and nothing but a slut."

"He's wrong."

"I know. You showed me that I'm a stronger woman. And I can be strong, yet want to give up control to the right man in the right circumstances." She swallowed. "I love you so much."

Her words caused his heart to skip a beat. "You love me?"

"I do." She leaned up and kissed him softly. "You are mine, Master Max."

"You belong to me Sierra, now and forever."

Thank you for reading Tempt the first book in the Wicked Sanctuary series. You'll see more of Max and Sierra in the next book, Entice as well learning more about Jordan and Crystal. If you enjoyed this book please consider leaving a review on Amazon, Goodreads or wherever you prefer, and know that it would be greatly appreciated.

For new release information and news about Marie Tuhart, please join her newsletter via her website.

Other books by Marie Tuhart

Her Desert Prince (Desert Destiny)
Her Desert Doctor (Desert Destiny)
Her Desert Horseman (Desert Destiny)
Her Desert Protector (Desert Destiny)
Highland Dom (McMillan Passion)
Bound & Teased
Claimed by the Sheikh
Billionaire's Cowboy's Conquest
More of You (Club Crave)
Reflections of you (Club Crave)
Bound to Love You (Club Crave)
Hot for You (Club Crave)

ABOUT THE AUTHOR

Marie Tuhart lives in the beautiful Pacific Northwest. Marie loves to read and write, when she's not writing, she spends time with family, traveling and enjoying life.

Marie is a multi-published author with The Wild Rose Press, Trifecta Publishing and self-publishing. To be alerted to her new releases you can join <u>Marie's newsletter</u> or check out her website at **w**ww.marietuhart.com.

Entice: A Wicked Sanctuary Novel
A preview

Chapter One

Crystal Hayden strode with confidence into Frost, Anderson, and Johnson law offices in Pleasant Valley. The firm was looking for a paralegal and she needed a job. Need was a strong word, she wanted this job. The grapevine said this could be a precedence setting case. So she set up an interview after talking to people she knew. They all had good things to say about the firm.

When the elevator pinged, Crystal stepped in and pushed the button for the third floor. She was itching to start a new job, a new challenge, a new opportunity. Being a freelance paralegal gave her the freedom to take jobs when she wanted. A case like this could further her career and make her a household name.

When she stepped out, her feet sank into a nice beige carpet as she made her way to the reception area. She was greeted by panic on the receptionist's face. Her hair in disarray.

Crystal moved closer. All the phone lines were blinking, files skewed everywhere. The young woman looked ready to run. She sat down her bag and went to help. "Answer the phone," Crystal said.

She picked up a file. Will, from her research that goes with an estate attorney. The next one a trust case, estate attorney. Family dispute, family law. Civil case about a property line, more than likely civil attorney.

Crystal looked up as the young woman hung up the phone, her hand pausing above it waiting for the next blinking light. When none comes, she slumps back in her chair.

"Thank you," she said. "I have no idea how this got out of control."

"No worries." One stack on the desk was done. There were four more to go. The phone rang, their brief respite ended. "Get the phone, I'll deal with these." Crystal indicated the pile of folders.

She'd spent far too much time filing and such when she'd first started working. Now she was at a level she didn't file unless she had to.

As the young woman kept answering the phone and taking messages, Crystal worked on each pile. The last pile was the easiest. The civil/criminal lawyer knew his stuff. He had everything set up already. All they needed was filing. Crystal liked this lawyer already.

"I'm Valerie." The young woman held out her hand in between calls.

"Crystal." After she shook Valerie's hand she waved at the stacks. "First two stacks are the family lawyer, the next one is will and estates, the last one is civil and criminal."

"You did that so fast." Valerie pushed a lock of her strawberry-blonde hair away from her face.

"You learn the tricks after a while. How long have you been doing this job?"

"Two weeks." Valerie blew out a breath.

"No wonder you're overwhelmed." The poor girl. "Would you mind some advice?" Crystal didn't want to presume.

"Oh yes, please. This is my first job, and I so want to do it right."

"Okay. Phones first. Taking messages and scheduling appointments are the most important thing. Filing is second. The trick is to file as soon as you get it if at all possible, and I would suggest, not having the files land on your desk." Crystal glanced to her left. "See the table over there? Get some bins and label them for each lawyer, then have them put their filing in there. Easier and cleaner."

"I never thought of that." Valerie smiled. "Thank you so much."

"You're welcome. You'll need to train the lawyers. They can be an unruly bunch."

"Yes, we can," a familiar male voice said to her right.

Crystal turned her head. "Jordan." What the heck was he doing here? Seeing one of the lawyers?

"Good morning, Crystal. I'm assuming you're the paralegal interviewing for the job?"

"Yes, but..." Crystal blew out a breath as it hit her. "You're part of this law firm." Damn it, why hadn't she remembered that. They'd talked discussed their jobs coffee a little over a month ago with her friends Sierra and Tessa. Funny how Christmas and New Year's had gone by in a blink of an eye.

"Guilty. Come on into my office." He gestured toward the door.

"I'm sorry, Mr. Frost, I didn't ask Crystal why she was here," Valerie said.

"No worries, Valerie, and remember, it's Jordan."

Crystal was happy Jordan wasn't angry at Valerie. She picked up her bag and swept past him, catching a whiff of his cologne. A woodsy scent that reminded her of hiking in the forest.

"Have a seat," Jordan said, closing the door behind him with a quiet click.

She gave his office the once over. Very nice. His desk was a light wood that contrasted with the dark wood bookcases and file cabinet. The chairs were a light brown, as was the sofa against one wall.

Pictures of the Space Needle, Narrows Bridge, Olympic Mountains, and Mt. Rainer graced his walls. Crystal sat down in one of the chairs in front of his desk. It was super comfy. Interesting. Most chairs were lacking in padding, not this one.

Crystal pulled out her resume, then sat her bag next on the floor against the chair.

"Thank you for helping Valerie. She's trying hard," Jordan said, a touch of amusement in his voice as he sat down. His leather chair let out a squeak.

"Of course. I've been there." Crystal shifted in her seat as he studied her with those brown eyes of his. "My resume," she said holding it out.

"Yes." He took the papers from her and set it down in front of him. His intense stare sent a wave of unease through her body. "Why do you want this job, Crystal?"

The husky tone of his voice sent shivers of awareness down her spine. She was a mass of contradiction. First unease, now awareness. He's a lawyer, she reminded herself. She wouldn't get involved with a lawyer, not again.

"The grapevine made it sound like a challenge." The ad hadn't said much. Paralegal wanted, experience with civil law a plus, temporary position for at least three months, possibly more.

"The grapevine?" He shook his head. "Figures, I wouldn't be able to keep this completely quiet and yes, it will be a challenge." He leaned back in his chair. "Are we going to have any issues working together?"

"I don't see why." She tilted her head.

"You were pretty upset with me after coffee."

Crystal looked down at her hands. Yeah, she'd been a bit curt with him. She blamed it on two parents arguing and their little boy looking so upset. How many times had that gone on when she was a child? How many times did an argument like that turn into a punishment?

"I'm sorry. I was upset. I shouldn't have taken it out on you."

"I can understand why it upset you. I dislike when parents air their issues in front of their kids, and I accept your apology." He rubbed his chin. "I trust you'll have no problem working with me."

"No, there's no reason I should." That was an odd question, even though they'd disagreed about talking to those parents.

"I want to make this clear. You'll be working for me."

A tremor went through her body. The way he said it made her think of late nights and midnight kisses. "What about the other two lawyers?" Thank goodness her voice was steady because her body was reacting to Jordan in ways it shouldn't be.

"They have a paralegal they share between them." Jordan leaned forward, his face serious. "I asked around when you made the appointment Crystal. You're one of the best paralegals in the field. I need someone like you."

This was interesting. He'd checked her out, not that she expected any less. "What is the case?"

"All I can say is it's a civil case, I can't go into particulars until we have a signed agreement and a non-disclosure in place."

Crystal's spine stiffened. "An NDA?" While it wasn't unheard of, her gut tensed. She was still wary of NDA's in the job place.

"Yes, this case is very sensitive."

"I see." She shifted in her seat. Sensitive. A shiver ran over her skin. Why was she reacting to him this way? It was like she'd never been attracted to someone before. Crystal took a deep breath and pushed her fascination aside. She didn't get involved with lawyers. "You said a temporary job for three months?"

"That is correct. I can tell you, a court date is set for two weeks from today. Preliminary one, so you're going to have your work cut out for you getting up to speed."

"Why did you wait so long to hire someone?" Another anomaly.

"Because I didn't think the case would get this far." He ran his hand over the back of his neck. "I'm in a bind and I hear you are the best. I'm willing to pay for that." He named a salary.

Crystal's mouth dropped. "You have to be kidding?" He had to be. No one paid that much. Yes, she knew her stuff, but seriously...she shook her head.

"I'm not. You're the best. You're not afraid of hard work or long hours. This salary takes that into account."

"It's far too much."

"I've never had anyone tell me I was paying them too much." The humor in his voice was apparent.

Crystal shrugged. "Being truthful."

"As I am. You're worth the money."

Another shiver racked her body at his husky tone. What was it about his voice? "All right. May I see the employment agreement?"

"Of course." He grabbed a folder and passed it to her.

Crystal opened it and began reading. "Sure of me, were you?" He already had her name filled in.

"Hopeful." He grinned at her.

That grin sent a tingle of awareness all the way to her toes. He's a lawyer, she reminded herself. The employment agreement was pretty standard. Crystal was still concerned about the money. She never argued that someone was paying her too much. "The NDA?"

Another folder was passed over to her. Crystal opened it and began reading. Pretty standard for most of it. There were a few areas that concerned her.

"I can't discuss the case with anyone at all?" That was a bit unusual.

"I have a list of professionals you can talk with about the case, but no one outside of that."

Crystal nodded. "What about the clause that says: *There may be incidents you see or talk about that are disturbing and different.* What kind of case is this?" The hair on the back of her neck stood up.

"Civil case. I can't say more than that."

She set the folders on his desk. "I understand your client's privacy, but I need to know more before I sign anything, so I can make an informed decision."

Jordan stared at her with those brown eyes. "How about this? Sign the NDA and I'll explain. Then, if you don't want to work on the case, no harm, no foul."

Crystal frowned. This was highly unusual. Her fingers twitched. What harm could there be in signing the NDA and finding out what the case was about?

His phone rang, and she jumped in her seat. She hadn't realized how quiet his office was.

"Excuse me, I need to take this."

Crystal nodded and began reading the NDA once more.

"Sage, I know." Jordan's voice was soft. "I'm working on it. You have to trust me. If you and Brady are seen together it will spell trouble in court." He paused. "Yes, I know you miss him and he wants to be with you."

Crystal glanced up to see the frustration on Jordan's face. Whatever the client was saying was not making him happy.

"The first court day is soon. Just hold on. Okay?" His features lightened. "Thank you. Yes, see you Thursday." He hung up the phone and looked at Crystal. "Sorry."

"Clients come first." Now that was an intriguing conversation. And, if it was tied to the case he wanted her working on, decision made. She plucked a pen from Jordan's desk and signed the NDA. She set the folder and the pen back on his desk. "Now tell me about this case."

Jordan smiled. "My client has been accused of abuse."

"Would that be criminal?"

"If the accuser was the one being abused, yes. In this case, it's his family."

"The accused is a woman?" Not that it couldn't happen. It was just surprising.

"My client is a woman. Everything that happens between my client and her s...boyfriend is consensual."

He'd stumbled over a word. Crystal wondered who the client was. "There's something you're not telling me."

"This is a very delicate situation. I know you're friends with Sierra, so how much has she told you about her and Max?"

"Probably everything. She and Max...Oh." The light bulb came on. "This involves someone in the kink community."

"Yes. I wasn't sure how much Sierra had shared."

"Only about how she's Max's submissive, and how much she enjoys him dominating her."

"Do you understand dominance and submission?"

"A little bit." Crystal shifted in her chair again. Jordan's eyes followed her slight shifting. A gleam lit his gaze and she forced herself to still. Of all the things she'd thought they'd talk about, this was not one of them. Was Jordan a Dom? Her body heated, wonder...Whoa, pull those thoughts back. She didn't date lawyers, remember.

"Before I go on about this case in particular, are you interested in kink?" He leaned forward in his chair and settled his elbows on his desk.

She froze in her seat. How to answer that? "Honestly, I'm not sure. I've read about it in romance books."

"No practical experience?"

"No." If her parents even thought she had impure thoughts, they'd punish her and put her in the sin room for days.

Jordan stood up and rounded his desk before leaning against it next to her chair. Crystal looked up at him. Her heart picked up at the smoldering look in his eyes.

"This case involves the kink community, if you haven't figured that out already. I need a paralegal that is open to doing the type of research that will include talking with others in the kink community."

"I can do that." Crystal force herself to breathe normally. Jordan was too close. Just like that night at the book club meeting and again at the coffee shop, his heat, his masculinity, called out to her. Her fingers tangled together in her lap.

"Can you?" He reached down and drew her to her feet. "I'm going to touch you, Crystal." When she didn't reply, he settled his hands loosely around her waist, moving with her when she stiffened.

"Wh-what are you doing?" Why did a quiver of anticipation flowed through her veins.

"Testing a theory." He widened his stance, leaned against his desk, and pulled her between his legs.

"This is unprofessional." While her tone was firm, her body melted against his. Why didn't she have any defense against him?

"You haven't signed the employee contract yet." He stared down at her. "Tell me, Crystal, have you ever wished to be tied up and at the mercy of a man you trusted in bed?"

A tremor shook her body within his embrace. "I refuse to answer on the basis I might incriminate myself." Who was she kidding? Only one boyfriend every tried that and she hadn't been able to stop giggling.

He grinned. "That's not an answer."

She squirmed in his hold. "Jordan, if you're going to be my boss, we can't do this." Oh but she wanted to. Where was her willpower? He was a lawyer and she'd promised herself after her last failed relationship with a lawyer that she would never get involved with anyone she worked with.

"This has nothing to do with your job and never will."

"I want that in the employment contract." The words came out before she could stop them.

His grin widened. "Done."

CPSIA information can be obtained
at www.ICGtesting.com
Printed in the USA
LVHW020043160520
655580LV00002B/311